Rachel felt a
Angel had just c
had been in her cabin while she was out. For the second time in the past few weeks someone had invaded her space.

Jesse took hold of her elbow and steered her toward the bed.

"You better sit down," he coaxed her. "You look pale and trembly."

Rachel sank down on the bed and stared around her.

"Jesse, what is going on? Why would someone come in here? I don't have anything valuable to steal."

"What about the pendant you found and gave to Maggie?" he suggested. His face was grim as he stood by Rachel.

"We better call Maggie. I think you should ask Kendall to let you and Angel stay in the main house until this is resolved."

Rachel didn't say a word. She just nodded and headed for the door. She didn't want to spend another minute in her cabin.

Books by Tina Ann Middleton

Mistaken Target
Nikki Dog
Love and Grace

Tina Ann Middleton

Tina Ann Middleton has written poems, essays, and stories since childhood. A voracious reader, she likes to ask, "what if?" and then spin stories from there. Tina describes herself as having an active (and sometimes overactive) imagination.

She and her husband, Darran, have been happily married since 1981 and have two grown daughters. Tina works at a VA Medical Center as administrative support in a Primary Care clinic and greatly enjoys serving Veterans.

She is the author of three independently published books, *Mistaken Target, Nikki Dog* and *Love and Grace.*

Follow Tina on Facebook and on Twitter -

https://www.facebook.com/tinaann.middleton

https://twitter.com/mid_tina

Cover design by Darran Middleton

The Forrestville Series
Book Two

Tina Ann Middleton

Publishing

ISBN-13: 978-1-7348336-2-1

Acknowledgments

When I wrote my first novel, *Mistaken Target*, it was going to be a stand-alone book. However, Jesse, who was introduced in *Mistaken Target*, needed to have his own story told. And, of course, he needed to meet his own special someone, who would need her story told as well.

Once again, I needed a lot of assistance with this project. I want to give heaps of thanks to all those who helped.

First, I want to thank my Heavenly Father for giving me the precious gift of being able to read and enjoy, as well as the ability to share my stories with others. Lord, everything I have is Yours; please use it for Your glory. Without You, Lord, I can do nothing. But with You, nothing is impossible – not even writing a four-book series.

My sweet husband Darran, I could not have done this project without you. You are my husband, my partner, and my friend. You are also the bringer of tea and coffee, and the one who spoils me rotten. I am in awe of the way you believe in me and my ability to write. I look forward to writing and publishing a lot of books together.

Kimberly, you have been of great help once again. Without your input, a couple of the fight scenes in this book would not have been right. Because of your help I was able to write scenes that are realistic and exciting. I'm so proud of how much you have learned and the level that you have reached in your martial arts training.

Many thanks to my friend, Shannon Mack. I so appreciate you allowing me to pick your brain on questions regarding legal and police matters for my story. Any mistakes or irregularities are purely mine.

My beta readers, Sharron Strawn and Virginia Disotell, I really appreciate you taking the time to read my book and provide input. Your encouragement and comments were incredibly helpful. Many thanks to both of you.

I also want to thank all the people who bought and read the first novel in the series. Without your support and encouragement, I don't know if I would've been able to write a second book. But now, because of your belief in me, there will be a four-book series.

The local chapter of the American Christian Fiction Writers has been so helpful to me. It is such an encouragement to be able to meet with other Christian writers and talk about our books, and more importantly, our common faith. Thank you for sharing your thoughts and your stories with me.

I am sure in all of these acknowledgments I have missed people who have played a vital part in the writing of this book. Let me say thank you now.

It takes more than an author to write a book. It takes the author, her family, her friends, and a multitude of others who provide encouragement and support. When you stir all that together, you come up with a book that will hopefully entertain and inspire others.

Tina Ann Middleton
November 2020

If we confess our sins, He is faithful and just to forgive us our sins and to cleanse us from all unrighteousness.

1 John 1:9 (NKJV)

Prologue

She had killed a man.

Rachel stared in disbelief at the limp body at her feet, her eyes wide with fear. She tried to check for a pulse in his neck, but her hands were shaking so hard she couldn't even turn the body over.

No one would believe it was self-defense. She was a domestic worker employed at the home of a wealthy man. The dead man was her employer's nephew, and probably his heir, since her employer had no children. Who would believe that she was trying to keep her victim from raping her?

Rachel tried to make herself move as she realized that she needed to get out of there before someone came looking for her or for the man whose life she had just taken. Her body felt leaden, however. She couldn't stop looking at the body on the floor. Finally, Rachel wrenched herself away from the scene.

She began throwing her belongings into a battered suitcase. As she tossed her clothes and toiletries into the suitcase, she didn't notice the small velvet pouch peeking out of a side pocket. Packing didn't take long since she lived simply, with few earthly goods.

Rachel allowed herself a moment's gratitude that she had been paid that day and had withheld some cash when she deposited her check while running errands. She hoped she could make a quick stop at an ATM to get more cash. Once she left the Austin area she would not use her ATM card again.

She forced herself to stop and take a few breaths so that she could remember what else she would need to take with her.

Groceries! Grabbing a plastic grocery bag, Rachel filled it with items that could be used for quick meals; things like peanut butter, crackers, fruit, cereal. She snatched up a cooler and dumped all the ice from her small freezer into it. Then she settled her eggs, milk, and a few other perishables in the ice.

Rachel gathered a couple of saucepans and her cast iron skillet, as well as plastic plates and a few utensils.

She had to stop several times to catch her breath from the sobs that shook her body as she worked. Everything and everyone that mattered to her were gone. Her father was dead. Her job was gone. Her reputation destroyed. Because she would be on the run, she could not stop to visit the one person she had left in this world.

Rachel carried her bags out to her small sedan, then hurried back into the cottage to check for anything she might have missed. Shudders shook her frame when she spotted the body slumped on her living room floor.

Tears ran down her cheeks as she gazed away from the scene to the cozy space that had been her home for several years.

Why had this happened to her?

Chapter One

Six hours earlier

Colin whistled softly as he moved through his new client's home. The spacious house was tastefully furnished and plainly stated the owner had money, and lots of it. This was Colin's favorite kind of place.

He made sure all the security devices were properly installed. Jacquelyn Marquette wanted the most up-to-date security to protect her belongings. Colin would make sure he gave her his best products and services. Then, right before he turned them on, he would help himself to something of hers.

It was all a game to him. Colin made plenty of money in his job, plus his family was wealthy. He didn't lack for anything he needed or wanted. He just liked the adrenaline rush of stealing and getting away with it.

Colin spied his prize as he moved into Ms. Marquette's bedroom. On a small desk, next to her laptop, there sparkled a red and gold enameled pendant shaped like a ladybug. The diamonds set in the middle and along the sides twinkled back at him. He grinned in anticipation and scooped it up, enjoying the weighty feel of the long thick chain attached to the ladybug. Colin found a small black velvet pouch and slipped the necklace into it to protect his prize, then tucked it in the pocket inside his suit.

He decided he would take this to his friend who owned a Dallas pawnshop when he made another one of his "business trips" next week. Of course, the only business Colin intended to conduct was to pawn his new treasure, then visit his favorite nightclub. Distracted by his plans, he didn't notice the small camera hidden in the far corner of his client's bedroom.

He checked the house one more time, then turned on the alarm system. His client had already told him what she wanted the password to be, so he didn't have to wait for her to come home to show her.

After leaving the house, Colin checked his watch.

"Colin, my boy," he spoke aloud as he wheeled out of the circular driveway. "You have done a good day's work. Time to reward yourself with a nice drink and maybe a pretty lady."

He pointed his car toward his favorite bar and turned up the radio as he sang along.

After a couple of hours and several drinks, Colin decided to head home. He was feeling very relaxed and satisfied with himself. Pulling into the driveway of his Uncle Marcus' estate, Colin spotted the small cottage allotted to the young cook who worked for his uncle.

Rachel James was a pretty little thing, with long auburn hair and soft brown eyes. She tended to be quiet and shy, but was an outstanding cook. Colin knew that his uncle, who was a well-known writer and historian, kept her busy with planning and cooking for dinners and social events. Colin enjoyed watching Rachel as she did her work, even though it was obvious that his presence made her nervous. He kind of liked keeping her off-balance like that.

Colin had tried flirting with the pretty young woman, but she maintained a quiet reserve that made it difficult.

This stung his pride, as he considered himself to be the kind of man any woman would want – young, handsome, wealthy.

He parked his car in front of what they called "the big house," then strolled, somewhat unsteadily, toward Rachel's cottage. He decided he would give the pretty little cook another chance to get to know him. Who knows? They might even become a couple. Colin snickered at the idea.

When he got to her door, he knocked lightly. When there was no answer Colin knocked more firmly. Still hearing no answer, he pulled a small toolkit from his pocket and extracted a thin metal blade, which he deftly manipulated in the lock. Colin heard a small snick that told him he had unlocked her door. With a satisfied grin he put his tools away and let himself in.

The empty cottage was sparsely furnished, with only a few personal belongings. Colin shook his head in amazement. He knew his uncle paid Rachel well, so why didn't she have more decorations and pretty things in her home? He poked around, being nosy, looking over all of her belongings. It didn't take long for the thief in him to get bored. Not only was there nothing worth stealing, there was nothing worth looking at, except for two framed photographs. One was a picture of a young couple with a baby. The other a picture of Rachel with two older men.

Colin picked up the second picture to study it for a moment. He could pick out Rachel's father since she strongly resembled him. Colin wondered idly who the other man was as he set the framed picture back in its place.

In front of the photographs he found a sturdy, decorative box with a floral design. He opened it to find an old tea cup and ceramic trinket box nestled in with a couple of scarves and some simple pieces of inexpensive jewelry.

Colin considered hiding the pendant in the box, but dismissed the idea. Rachel might want something from the box before he could get back to it.

Peeking in the bedroom closet, Colin found a battered suitcase. This would be perfect for hiding the necklace. Colin didn't want to risk keeping it in his jacket pocket. The last time he did that, he forgot the item in his pocket until his jacket was washed. That had required some hasty explaining. Colin still wasn't sure his uncle had accepted his story of how the item had ended up in his pocket.

He heard footsteps in the gravel drive and realized it was about time for Rachel to come home. Quickly he slipped the necklace, which was still in its pouch, in an inside pocket of the suitcase. He would come back for it the next day while she was at work. Hearing Rachel's key in the door, he shoved the suitcase back and stepped out of her bedroom.

Rachel sighed, tired from a long day of work. She planned to eat a light dinner and go to bed before nine o'clock. She had gotten up at dawn and worked hard all day preparing for a dinner party the next night. She wanted to be well-rested for the extra work that she needed to do before the party.

She paused to look around her and enjoy the beauty of the late spring day. Rachel's father, Matthew James, had always loved spring. He said it reminded him of when God created the world. Her father had loved watching nature come to life – trees greening out, flowers blooming.

Tears came to Rachel's eyes. She couldn't believe it was only a little over a year since he had died in the car crash that also severely injured his older brother, Jonathan.

Rachel felt a wave of gratitude toward her employer for providing her cottage and meals. Since her basic needs were already met, Rachel could afford to send most of her generous paycheck to the rehab facility where Uncle Jon was recovering.

Rachel reached to insert her key in the cottage door, but found it was already unlocked. She thought she had locked it that morning. Rachel tried to remember if she had, but all she could recall was that she had been in a hurry to get to work. She shook her head and pushed the door open.

Rachel's heartbeat stuttered when she saw a man leaning against the doorway to her bedroom. She felt a chill come over her when she recognized Colin. She usually tried to be polite to him, but the man made her nervous.

He constantly flirted with her, touching her hand or shoulder. Sometimes he stood very close when he talked to her. Rachel had even considered talking to Mr. Taylor and asking him to intervene. But Colin was his nephew, so she hesitated to complain about him.

"Good evening, Rachel."

Colin's grin was crooked and his steps unsteady as he moved toward her, emanating an odor of whiskey. The pungent odor caused Rachel to step back, instinctively moving toward the door. Should she leave the cottage or ask him to leave?

"What? No greeting for me?"

Colin leaned past her and closed the door, then ran his finger over Rachel's smooth cheek. She recoiled, her skin crawling at his touch.

"Mr. Taylor, what are you doing in my cottage?"

Rachel was frightened and angry. She was tired of this man harassing her with his attentions. Now he had invaded her home.

"Mr. Taylor's my uncle," he crooned as he reached for her arms. "Call me Colin."

"*Mr. Taylor*," she emphasized as she stepped away from him, "I would like for you to leave now."

Colin's grin disappeared.

"What's the matter?" he snarled. "I'm not good enough for you?"

Rachel slid to the side to evade him, but he pursued her, the glint in his eyes announcing his intent. When Colin reached to grab her again, Rachel dropped to the floor and stretched out her leg, sweeping it behind his feet. Colin fell heavily, almost striking his head on a corner of her coffee table.

He struggled to his feet, a leering grin filling his face. "You like to play rough, huh?"

Rachel bolted behind a chair, then the kitchen table, as the drunken man tracked her around the cottage. Her stomach lurched when she heard him giggling as if they were children playing a game.

Finally, he grabbed her again and she seized his arm in a firm grip and twisted it behind him. The giggles disappeared and he filled the air with profanity-laced threats of what he would do to her when he got free.

Rachel felt terror overwhelm her when he nearly pulled free from the arm hold. Pulling him close, she wrapped her arm around Colin's neck and applied pressure. This was a maneuver her father and Uncle Jon taught her to use only if *absolutely* necessary.

But Rachel was in full panic mode. She wasn't thinking about her training or about using caution. Her skin crawled at the idea that if Colin got free, he would rape her. He might even kill her. In that state of mind, she didn't think at all, she simply reacted.

Colin's attempts to get away became increasingly feeble until they stopped altogether. Rachel was so focused on protecting herself that it took a moment for her to realize that he had gone limp. She came to herself with a start.

What had she done?!

Chapter Two

Rachel swiped at the tears still rolling down her cheeks. An hour of driving had not lessened the shock and fear. Just when she thought she had managed to think about something else, her mind would revert to the sight of Colin Taylor's body slumped on her living room floor.

Uncle Jon had warned her repeatedly her lack of self-control could result in a serious injury to someone if she had to defend herself, but Rachel had never imagined that she could kill someone.

They'll never believe me! The desperate thought echoed in an endless loop. They'll never believe I was just defending myself. He's the nephew of a famous and wealthy historian. Probably his heir. I'm just a lowly menial worker.

"Oh, God! What am I going to do?"

Rachel had grown up in church, but didn't really think about God that often. Church was just a habit; one that she had given up after her father died the year before. She prayed for her uncle from time to time. Mostly she just worked hard and sent the lion's share of her check to the rehab facility for Uncle Jon's treatment.

A siren sounded behind her, growing louder as it approached. Rachel tensed and eased the car to the right. She expected any minute that the police car would pull in front of her and the officer would get out and point his gun at her. Rachel held the steering wheel in a death grip until the squad car passed her with the siren still wailing.

Rachel blew out a huge sigh of relief and eased her hold on the steering wheel. She knew she had to set aside her shock and fear so that she could plan. Spotting a sign for a dollar store, she exited and pulled into the parking lot.

She clipped her long hair up and checked to make sure no sign of tears showed. Rachel didn't want the store personnel or other customers to have any reason to remember her. As she entered the store, she grabbed a basket and began her shopping. A plan formed while she picked up the supplies she needed - hair color, scissors, a couple of ball caps, some jeans and t-shirts.

Rachel headed for the checkout after stopping at the end of an aisle to pick up a few snacks. She greeted the cashier with a brief hello and a small smile. She didn't want the cashier to remember her for anything; so she made sure she was not too friendly or too remote. Just nice and casual, she reminded herself.

After she checked out, Rachel drove until she found a small motel. Before getting out of the car, she grabbed one of her new baseball caps and a pair of sunglasses. She wound her hair into a tight coil and secured it, then jammed the cap on top, making sure none of her hair showed.

Although it was after 7:00 in the evening, there was still plenty of sunlight, so Rachel wasn't worried about looking strange wearing the sunglasses in the evening.

She reached in the backseat for her suitcase and the bags from the dollar store. Juggling her load, Rachel arrived in the lobby of the motel feeling very warm and slightly out of breath.

The motel clerk hardly seemed to notice her. He nudged the ledger toward Rachel for her signature, then handed her the key and told her where to find the room. His eyes never seemed to leave the novel he was reading while he gave her the information in a monotone.

Rachel hefted her suitcase and the bag from the dollar store onto the bed. She looked around the small room with satisfaction. It wasn't fancy by any means, but it was clean and quiet. She felt it would be just right.

She looked at the bag and sighed. Time to get to work. She opened her suitcase and grabbed her scissors. Taking a deep breath and grabbing a section of her waist-length hair, she ruthlessly cut it off, finally finishing with her hair bobbed just above her shoulders.

Rachel had worn her hair long since she was a small child. Cutting it off was almost as painful as cutting one of her arms off, she thought. But it was necessary.

When she was satisfied with her new haircut, Rachel carefully read the directions on the box of hair color before beginning the process. When she stepped out of the shower and dried her hair, it was no longer the dark auburn she had grown up with. Now it was a plain medium brown. Rachel examined her new look critically. She wanted to make sure she looked nothing like her former self.

Although she was not really hungry, Rachel forced herself to eat a light supper. As she ate, she watched the local news. She wanted to know if Colin's body had been found yet and if the police were looking for her.

To her surprise, there was no mention of a death or a manhunt. Rachel guessed that no one had found him yet. She wondered if she should call in an anonymous tip, then decided against it. If Colin had not been found yet, that would give her more time to get away.

After finishing her dinner, Rachel sat on the bed and brushed her hair. She missed the length she was used to. As her hands performed the rhythmic motion, her mind wandered.

"Daddy, help!"

The little girl's hands were wrapped around a large tangle in her long brown hair. It seemed the more she tried to untangle it, the worse it got. Her little hands and arms were getting tired.

Her father took the detangling comb from her.

"Turn around," he instructed her.

With her back turned to him, her father gently untangled the knots and combed her hair. When the comb ran through smoothly, he turned her around and handed the comb to her.

"There you go, sweetheart."

He gave her a tight hug, then looked down into her small face.

"You look so beautiful. Just like your mother."

Rachel loved hearing that from him. To her, being compared to her mother was a high compliment. She squeezed her arms around his middle.

"I love you, Daddy. Thank you for helping me."

He gave her a big smile and returned the squeeze.

"I love you too, princess. You're welcome. You can always come to me for help."

Rachel found that she was crying again.

"Oh, Daddy, I wish I could come to you now."

The next morning, Rachel checked out early and made sure to wear the baseball cap and sunglasses again. The morning clerk gave her a friendly greeting and accepted her payment with a smile. As she pulled out of the motel parking lot, Rachel pondered her next step. She looked down at the steering wheel and realized she needed to get rid of this vehicle since it would be recognized as hers.

When Rachel saw a sign for a used car dealership, she exited the interstate and made her way onto the lot. She parked near the building, then wandered the rows of cars and trucks. Her little sedan was still fairly new, so she felt she could get a good trade in. But she needed to find something that would be completely different from what she would be expected to drive.

At the back of the lot was a row of older vehicles. About halfway down the row sat a little blue pickup truck. It had a few rust spots, but to Rachel's inexperienced eyes, it seemed the perfect solution. No one would expect her to be driving a truck.

One of the salesmen saw her looking at the truck and hurried to her side.

"Hi! I'm Jim. Can I help you find something?"

Rachel shook his hand and smiled, but did not give her name.

"I would like to see this truck. Can I sit in it?"

She watched the salesman try to hide his disappointment. The truck was one of the lowest-priced vehicles on the lot. He wouldn't get much of a commission from it. She could see when he decided that a sale was a sale as he swallowed and gave her a friendly grin.

"Sure! Just let me get the keys."

The salesman hurried into the building, reappearing almost immediately. He handed Rachel the jingling keyring.

Sliding inside the truck, Rachel tried to look it over thoroughly. She didn't know much about cars and how they work, but she could tell if someone had taken care of it.

The truck was clean inside; no spills or stains showing. She sniffed the air in the cab and noticed it did not smell smoky or musty. That was something in its favor.

Rachel thanked the salesman as she slid out of the truck.

"I really like this little truck. Do you take trade-ins?"

"Yes, ma'am. What do you have?"

She pointed to her little sedan sitting near the office building. It was not fancy, but was well-cared for. Rachel was glad that she had washed the car the week before.

After a little dickering about how much they'd give her for her car and how much they wanted for the truck, Rachel drove out of the dealership with her first truck. She was uncomfortable with the fact that she had had to use her name on the paperwork and hoped that wouldn't lead law enforcement right to her.

"I'm not going to stay in this area anyway," she said aloud as she drove away. Still, the thought stayed with her. She hoped this wasn't a mistake that would lead to her arrest.

Rachel drummed her fingers on the steering wheel as she waited for the traffic to move again. Construction on the interstate combined with careless driving had led to a fender bender down the road. Now traffic was at a standstill.

She looked at the cones and barrels around her and shook her head in amazement. Rachel remembered coming this way on road trips with her father when she was a little girl. The highway had been under construction then too.

Rachel took advantage of the paused traffic flow to take a long drink from her water bottle.

"I wonder if Texas just keeps I-35 in a permanent state of construction," she muttered as she inched her truck forward.

Rachel held her breath when she got to the scene of the accident and a state trooper waved her through. She tried to look nonchalant, but feared guilt was stamped on her face. The officer, however, paid no attention to her other than to motion for her to drive on. Rachel didn't release the breath until she was several yards past him.

She passed the exit in Temple that she always took to visit the rehab facility and sighed; her heart heavy. Rachel would love to visit Uncle Jon and tell him everything that happened. She knew that he would comfort and encourage her, no matter what she had done. But Rachel was afraid that law enforcement would be waiting for her if she went. It was not a secret that her uncle was in that facility and that she visited him on a regular basis.

Rachel felt the sting of tears in her eyes. She was so scared and lonely. She felt cut off from everyone she cared about. Why had this happened to her?

To distract herself, Rachel began looking for an exit where she could make a bathroom stop and get a cup of coffee and a snack. Or maybe just the coffee, she thought. Buying the truck had taken a big bite out of her cash supply. She would need to be very careful about how she spent her money.

She drove all day, headed north on I-35. That evening she entered Oklahoma and stopped for the night at a rest stop.

Grabbing her pillow and blanket, Rachel tried to get comfortable in the back of the truck. She felt she could not afford to stay at motels very often. She would sleep in the truck as much as possible.

The next morning, Rachel woke from an uneasy sleep and groaned. The truck bed was a hard and bumpy surface to try to rest on. In addition to the physical discomfort, she was nervous. Every time she heard a noise, she would jolt awake, then lie still listening until she was sure it was safe to go back to sleep.

After getting out of her uncomfortable sleeping place, Rachel forced herself to stretch and walk a bit before she got behind the wheel and went in search of a public rest room where she could freshen up.

For the next several days Rachel wandered the highways and back roads of southern Oklahoma. There were several small towns where she considered stopping to look for work and settling down. But Rachel still felt restless and uneasy. She decided to head for Louisiana.

If only she could find a place where she felt safe.

Chapter Three

Colin struggled back to consciousness. His head pounded and he felt like he was going to be sick. He had had hangovers before, but this felt like the king of hangovers. Even his neck felt sore. Wait, why was his neck sore? That had never happened before when he drank.

He sat up and gingerly explored with his fingers. His neck felt tender and bruised. Colin tried to remember what had happened. As he looked around, the memories rushed into place. He was in Rachel's cottage. He had come in, hidden the necklace and waited for Rachel. She rebuffed him. He got angry with her. Then she had held him around the neck until he lost consciousness.

Colin stood up and glanced around the small living space. It looked as if someone had packed in a hurry and left. All of the rooms were cleaned out. Then he remembered . . .THE NECKLACE! He stumbled to the bedroom, almost falling in his haste, and searched in the closet. The suitcase was gone, with his prize still tucked inside.

He slammed the closet door and swore. Rachel had packed her stuff and left while he was unconscious. Now he had to explain to his uncle why the pretty little cook was gone. He had also lost out on the money he would have gotten for the necklace.

Colin staggered into the living room and plopped down on the couch, where he sat and held his aching head. He tried to think what he needed to do next.

He decided that when Uncle Marcus told him Rachel was gone, he would act surprised. His uncle never needed to know that Colin had been in Rachel's cottage. As for the pendant, well, there was still lots of stuff out there to steal.

He got excited just thinking about it.

"Come in, Mr. Taylor. Ms. Marquette is expecting you."

The thickly-muscled man towering over Colin seemed an odd choice for a maid or receptionist, but he was the one who had answered the door before Colin could even ring the bell or knock.

Colin followed the man upstairs to Jacquelyn Marquette's home office. He thought she probably wanted to thank him in person for doing such a good job with her security. Colin knew he was good at his job and believed others thought the same about him.

He took the proffered chair and looked up to see his client studying him.

Jacquelyn Marquette was a beautiful woman with long black hair, a porcelain-like complexion, and startling blue eyes. She dressed in professional attire, but somehow managed to convey an intensely feminine and alluring impression. Colin felt a spark of attraction and thought about asking her out on a date. The first words out of her mouth, however, threw cold water on any ideas of romance with this client.

"Mr. Taylor, why did you steal from me?"

Colin bolted upright in the chair and stared at her in horror. How could she have known? He had not turned the security system, with its strategically placed cameras, on until after he had pocketed the necklace. She must be guessing.

"Ms. Marquette, I am horrified that you would even consider me as someone who would steal from you. Trust is vital in my business."

Now Colin felt he was back in control.

"I am so sorry that something was stolen from you. What was the item? Perhaps we can check the cameras and catch the thief."

Jacquelyn just gazed at him; her blue eyes unreadable. Then she motioned to the man who greeted Colin at the door.

"Brock, please start the video from *my* cameras."

Colin felt something clench in his stomach and thought he was going to be sick. He didn't know she had had her own cameras set up. He didn't see them when he set up the system she had bought from his company. How could he have missed that?

Colin felt perspiration begin to bead on his forehead. He took out his handkerchief and blotted his face, then looked up at the screen.

The camera showed Colin entering the bedroom and stepping over to Jacquelyn's desk. It gave a clear view of him picking up the pendant, admiring it, then putting it in the pouch and sliding them into his jacket's inside pocket.

Colin felt Jacquelyn's eyes on him again. He tried to come up with an explanation, but he had none. He was caught and that was all there was to it.

"Mr. Taylor, I will ask you again."

Jacquelyn's voice sent a chill over Colin.

"Why did you steal from me?"

He hung his head and tried his best to look remorseful.

Colin gave Jacquelyn a pitiful look in an attempt to make her feel sorry for him.

"I'm sorry, Ms. Marquette. It's a real problem that I cannot seem to get rid of. I get this overwhelming compulsion to steal. I have tried and tried to overcome it. I've even been to counseling, but it didn't do any good."

Colin peeked up to see if she was buying it. She had a pensive look on her face. He felt hopeful. Maybe he would get away with it, after all.

Finally, Jacquelyn sighed.

"Actually, I don't really care about the *why*. The only reason I asked you was so that you would know I saw you steal from me."

Jacquelyn stood up and leaned over her desk, capturing Colin's eyes with her own gaze which bored into him.

"I do care about getting back what was stolen from me. If you will return the pendant, I will be satisfied, though I never want to have anything to do with you again. I can't abide people who steal from me."

She looked at him with a sinister smile.

"If you don't return my property, I will make you wish you had never had anything to do with me. I don't call the police. I take care of things myself. Return the pendant or I will kill you – slowly and painfully."

Colin felt his stomach sink. The pendant was gone with Rachel and he had no way of finding her. He believed that Jacquelyn would do what she threatened. Colin knew he couldn't go to the police for protection. They would put him away for theft.

"I don't know where the necklace is," he finally admitted. He told her about putting the pendant in a suitcase, planning to return for it later. He didn't mention the incident with Rachel defending herself from him, just that the person the suitcase belonged to had left town unexpectedly, taking the necklace too.

"You will find this woman," Jacquelyn spoke calmly, but Colin heard the menace in her words.

"You will find my necklace that you stole and you will return it to me. Do you understand?"

Colin nodded, his heart racing. He didn't know how he would find Rachel, but he had to start searching. He tore his eyes from her icy gaze as he got up and turned to leave.

"One more thing, Mr. Taylor."

Jacquelyn had seated herself again and was scribbling on a business card, which she held out to him.

"You will call me each week with an update of your search. If you fail to call me, I will send Brock to find you."

She smiled sweetly, a startling contrast to the next words she uttered.

"I don't think you want Brock to come find you."

"Colin, I need to speak with you for a few minutes. Let's go in my study."

The young man tensed. He knew what Uncle Marcus wanted to talk to him about – Rachel's disappearance. The grounds keeper had seen him enter her cottage and had blabbed about it to his uncle. Now Colin had to come up with a reason he was in Rachel's cottage.

"Uncle Marcus, how did your research go today?"

Colin hoped he could get his uncle off of the uncomfortable topic of Rachel by asking about the book the historian was working on. But Marcus Taylor could not be distracted that easily. He settled at his desk and motioned for his nephew to sit in one of the comfortable leather chairs in front of him.

"Do you know why Rachel left so abruptly without giving notice or talking to me? Did she say anything to you?"

Colin thought about making up a story about a sick relative of Rachel's, then realized his uncle might be able to help him find Rachel. If he could find her, he could find the necklace; something he did *not* plan to mention to Marcus.

"No sir, I have no idea why she left. We chatted a bit the evening she left, but she didn't say anything about leaving. Her sudden departure without giving notice makes me very concerned that she might be in some kind of trouble and needs our help. Do you know how we might search for her?"

Colin watched his uncle to see if he would believe him. He had some ideas about how to search for Rachel, but he wanted his uncle's help too. Marcus Taylor was an influential man with contacts all over the country. It was possible someone the historian knew would be able to aid in the search.

Jacquelyn Marquette's threat to kill him if he did not return her property terrified Colin. After his talk with her, he had returned to his office and asked around to learn what he could about the woman. After hearing what his coworkers had to tell him about her ruthlessness, he wished he had not taken the security assignment.

They didn't know about the stolen necklace, and Colin wasn't about to tell them. But they told him stories that showed she was a cold hard woman who would do whatever she thought necessary for her own success. The look on her face when she told him she would kill him slowly and painfully haunted his dreams. He had to get that necklace back -NOW!

He came out of his reverie to see his uncle studying him with suspicion. Then Marcus nodded.

"I think I may have some resources to find Rachel. We'll find out if she is in trouble and if she needs or wants our help."

Marcus regarded his nephew sternly.

"But, if I find you did anything to frighten her away, we're going to have a short, hard talk which will probably end with you leaving here. Understood?"

Colin sagged in relief, then caught himself. He put a worried look on his face, which wasn't very hard. He *was* worried. He was worried about himself and what Jacquelyn would do to him if he didn't return that necklace.

"I understand, Uncle Marcus. I'll do anything you say to help find her."

Chapter Four

Rachel rubbed her stomach as it growled, reminding her that she had been driving for hours and was starving. Just as she crossed into Louisiana she spotted a rest area and flipped on her turn signal. Pulling beside a small picnic table and parking, she sat for a moment to check out her surroundings. So far it looked like she had the picnic area to herself.

She parked and opened her door. Gravel crunched under her shoes as she pulled the seat forward to get to her small cooler. Rachel carried the cooler to the table and sorted through it for the ingredients to make a sandwich. She laid them out on a paper towel that she had spread on the table.

While Rachel sat and munched on her bologna sandwich, she thought about her flight. She yawned in between bites and wished she could go somewhere and get a good night's sleep.

As she bit into an apple, Rachel shook her head at herself. Most fugitives, she thought, would have had a destination and would have hightailed it straight to that point. She, however, once she had left the Austin area, wandered aimlessly. So far, she had not seen anything to indicate that law enforcement was looking for her. She smiled grimly.

They would be looking for a sweet, feminine young woman with long auburn hair, wearing a dress and pumps. Instead, she was dressed in jeans, t-shirt, and sneakers. The ball cap had become a major part of her wardrobe.

Movement to her right caught her eye and made her realize she had not been paying attention to her surroundings. Her father and Uncle Jon would have reprimanded her, telling her she knew better.

"Always know your surroundings, Rachel. You never know who or what might be in the shadows or hiding behind an object. Keep your senses on alert at all times."

Turning her head to see what had moved allowed Rachel to see a medium-size dog tentatively approaching, its nose quivering at the scent of the bologna still sitting on the picnic table.

Rachel had a soft spot in her heart for animals and the dog's pitiful condition broke her heart.

"You hungry, little one?" she asked softly.

She took a piece of bologna from the package, tore off a piece, and offered it to the hungry animal.

The dog approached Rachel, and got just close enough that it could stretch its neck out and grab the bologna from Rachel's fingers. After inhaling the lunch meat, it looked hopefully up at Rachel, who laughed and held out the rest of the slice of bologna. The dog inched a little closer and tried to take the meat.

Rachel held the food back a little in an attempt to coax the dog a bit closer. As she watched the poor creature eat, she could see through the dirty black and white matted coat that it was a female. Rachel reached out slowly and let the dog sniff her hand. The dog sniffed for a moment, then licked Rachel's fingers. Rachel ran her hand down the dog's head and back, then scratched her behind the ears.

The dog wagged her tail in appreciation, then turned her head to stare at the trash barrel for a moment. Her ears were up, as if she heard something Rachel did not hear. Rachel looked around again, but did not see what had caught the dog's attention.

After stroking on the stray for a few minutes, Rachel cleaned up from her lunch, then headed toward the large trash barrel with her lunch remains. There was a blur of black and white as the dog jumped between Rachel and the barrel, barking and blocking Rachel's forward progress.

Startled, Rachel stopped and stared at the dog. The young female did not seem aggressive, just determined to not let Rachel move in that direction.

"What's wrong with you, crazy dog?" she demanded. "I need to throw this stuff away and get on the road."

She took another step toward the trash receptacle, but the dog barked again and stared into Rachel's eyes as if trying to tell her something. Her little body stayed firmly planted between Rachel and the barrel.

Rachel shook her head and laughed.

"You seem very determined to keep me from throwing away my trash."

Then she had an idea.

"Are you still hungry? Do you want some more to eat?"

She dug in the bag of groceries and fished out another couple of pieces of bologna and a piece of bread. Rachel tossed these on the ground in the opposite direction of the trash can, hoping to distract the dog long enough to let her take care of her trash and get in the truck.

It didn't work. The dog didn't even take her eyes off of Rachel, although she licked her chops at the scent of the food.

Rachel took another step forward, hoping the dog

would not become aggressive. Suddenly she heard a rattling sound. Concentrating on the grass under the trash can, she saw the mound of coils attached to the rattle. The little stray had saved her from a rattlesnake!

Fighting a surge of nausea at how close she had come to being bitten, Rachel backed away and sank down on the picnic bench. Her head swam as she realized that she could have died if that dog had not been so determined to keep her away from that hidden snake.

"Come here, girl," Rachel called.

The young dog trotted over from eating the food Rachel had thrown to distract her and happily accepted Rachel's head scratch.

"You saved my life, you know. I think you must be my guardian angel."

After catching her breath from her near disaster, Rachel gathered up her things again and headed for the truck. She decided to just drop her trash in a garbage can the next time she gassed up. She wasn't even going to try to approach another trash barrel, especially with the tall grass and weeds growing around them.

When she opened the passenger door to stow her things in the back, the dog scurried behind her and jumped up, settling into the driver's seat with a paw on the steering wheel, and looking very pleased with herself.

Rachel started to tell her to get out, then stopped as she thought of something. Maybe having the dog along would be a good idea. With the dog along to let her know if anyone approached, maybe Rachel could get a good night's sleep.

"I think I'll call you Angel," she told her new dog. "How would you like to ride along with me and be my guardian angel?"

Angel barked her approval and washed Rachel's face. Rachel laughed and rubbed her head. Then she wrinkled her nose when she caught a whiff of dirty dog.

"I think the first thing we need to do is get you a bath and a good brushing."

Angel whimpered and laid her head on the truck seat, looking pitiful.

Rachel just laughed as she got in the truck and drove away from the rest area. Somehow, she felt better having her new friend.

"Come on, baby," Rachel crooned with a desperate note in her voice.

"You can do it. Just a little further, please."

Angel raised her head from the truck seat and gave her owner a quizzical look. Rachel knew her dog was puzzled at her tone since it was the same one she often used for the Border Collie. She couldn't stop to reassure the dog now, though.

The old truck had been threatening to overheat for all morning. Rachel had stopped several times to refill the radiator and let the engine cool. As she passed a sign that read "Welcome to Forrestville," the needle on the temperature gauge was well into the red and smoke was pouring from under the hood.

Rachel tried to urge the truck a little further so that she could at least pull into the nearby service station, but the vehicle could go no further and stopped on the street, right behind another pick-up truck parked in front of a hardware store. Despite her desperate attempts to restart the engine, Rachel knew her truck was not moving from that spot unless someone pushed it.

She pulled a lever, then got out to raise the hood and let the engine cool. While she waited for the smoke to clear, Rachel glanced around with interest.

Forrestville seemed to be a pretty, well-kept small town. Wide sidewalks with trees and flower-filled concrete planters wound by attractive storefronts that invited passers-by to window shop. A candy store sent out a tempting aroma of chocolate that competed with the scent of fried chicken that floated from the diner down the road. Rachel's stomach growled as she realized that she had not eaten since the night before, when she finished off her small store of groceries.

Deciding that she had a more urgent situation at the moment, Rachel tried to peer under the hood. She had no idea what she was looking for or how to get her truck going again.

Resisting the urge to slam the hood in anger, Rachel decided her best option was to go in the hardware store and ask for help moving the vehicle to the nearby service station. If no one inside could help, then she'd walk over to the station for help.

"Angel, stay," she commanded.

The dog whined, then laid her head on the seat. Rachel left the window half-way down so her companion would have some cool air, then headed into the store.

Angel sat up and looked around. When she spotted a young man across the street, she quietly jumped through the window and sprinted across the street to intercept him.

Jesse ran through his mental checklist as he strode down the sidewalk. He had just a couple more errands to complete before he met David and Christy Michaels at

Mary Ann's Diner for lunch. After that, he needed to get back to the Rocking K ranch for afternoon chores.

The magnitude of God's grace and mercy never ceased to amaze the young man. After confessing to selling drugs for a local businessman, Jesse had expected to spend several years in prison. But, because he had also provided crucial testimony against the drug lord and had saved him from a grieving father who tried to kill the man who destroyed his son, Jesse's sentence had been suspended.

Jesse stood listening to the stern voice of the judge as he read Jesse the riot act for his part in the selling of cocaine to young people. Gratitude and amazement flooded him when Maggie Jones, the Police Chief for Forrestville, came forward to speak up for him. Several other members of the community stood to support him as well.

"Young man," the judge told him. "You have done a great wrong. But you also have demonstrated that you are remorseful and ready to change. In light of your changed attitude and the assistance you have provided in apprehending and providing testimony against the man leading the drug ring in Forrestville, I will suspend your sentence and place you on probation for five years. You will not work in your former job for the town of Forrestville as I do not want you in the same environment you were in during your drug dealing time. In addition, you will also be under the watchful eye of your own police chief. I believe Chief Jones will help you walk the straight and narrow."

Maggie was the one who told him about the Rocking K ranch and introduced him to the owner, Kendall Ford. He remembered the kind look in the woman's eyes as she shook his hand with a firm grip. Kendall had let him know he was welcome, but he would have to work hard and be accountable to her. After three years at the ranch, Jesse could not imagine working anywhere else, unless it was his own ranch. That was a dream for the future, however.

Jesse brought his mind back to the present as he headed to his next stop on his mental list. He was almost finished, then he could go to lunch. As he was debating if he wanted fried chicken or a hamburger, he was stopped short by a medium-size black and white dog standing in front of him. The little female just stood and stared into his eyes.

"Well, hello, little dog."

Jesse knelt down and held out his hand for the Border Collie to sniff. She gave him a quick sniff and lick on his hand, but stayed firmly planted in front of him. Jesse stood and tried to walk around the little dog, but she moved into his path and gave a short bark, as if commanding him to do something.

"Sorry, girl, I don't have anything for you."

Jesse tried again to move around her, but the collie simply stepped in front of him and barked again. Then she moved toward him, her gaze into his eyes still steady.

It occurred to Jesse that the dog wanted him to go somewhere. He had seen Border Collies in action, herding cattle or sheep. This dog was acting like she was herding him!

Jesse looked in the direction the dog seemed to be trying to move him and saw the beat-up truck, with the hood up and engine smoking, parked right behind his pick-up. He felt the anger rise inside him as he strode to look closer.

"Why is this piece of junk sitting behind my truck?!" he shouted.

He looked around in an attempt to find the owner.

"Who left this rust bucket sitting here?" he demanded again.

"That 'piece of junk' is my only means of transportation,"

a female voice responded. "And it is sitting there because that's where it died."

Jesse found himself in front of a young woman with short, medium-brown hair that was covered by a baseball cap. Her brown eyes sparked with annoyance that he realized was aimed at him. But he was feeling pretty irritated himself.

"I can see why it died," he snapped. "I'm surprised it ran in the first place."

He looked around and saw an open bay at the service station a few yards down the road.

"You couldn't get it a little further down the road to Willy's?"

The young woman looked confused at the name until she saw the direction he was looking. A wave of red washed over her face.

"No," she bit out. "The truck didn't want to go that far. I was just inside trying to find someone to help me push it, but couldn't find any volunteers under the age of 80."

Jesse began to feel ashamed of himself. He wasn't being very welcoming to this visitor to his town who needed help. Not really ready to admit he was wrong, he abruptly turned to the dog, who was sitting in the truck, watching the conversation.

"Your dog seems to think I can help you," he retorted. Jesse couldn't help the small grin that crept onto his face. "She came and got me to help you. Wouldn't let me past her."

Rachel turned her eyes to her companion, who gazed back at her innocently. Remembering how Angel had behaved at the rest stop, she could believe the dog had herded this rude man over to her truck. He was good-looking, but did he have to be so, so annoying?

She looked back at him, noticing the tanned arms and face and the black hair that curled at the back of his neck. His brown eyes danced with humor; the annoyance that had flashed from them faded now.

"Come on," he offered. "You steer and I'll push you over to Willie's."

Rachel nodded and slammed the hood on the truck. She murmured her thanks as she slid behind the wheel, shoving Angel back into the passenger seat. Angel laid her head on the seat with a satisfied expression on her doggy face. Rachel looked down at her.

"You think you're so smart, don't you?"

"Did you say something?" Jesse called from the back of the truck.

Embarrassed, Rachel just waved at him as she put the truck in neutral and steered toward the local service station.

"Welcome to Willie's Service Station," the mechanic greeted them. "Where service is what we do best. I'm Willie."

Rachel bit back a grin as she watched Jesse try not to roll his eyes. She assumed he had heard this line quite a few times.

She extended her hand to the mechanic.

"I'm Rachel James. I appreciate whatever you can do for my poor truck. But I don't have much money. Can we work out a payment plan?"

It was hard for her to admit her inadequate financial status, but Rachel didn't want to start something she couldn't pay for.

Willie narrowed his eyes as he studied her.

"You're new in town, aren't you? You got a job?"

"N...not yet. But I think I can find one pretty easily."

Rachel felt her face flaming as if she was lying. She did believe she could find something, even if it was temporary. She felt the men's scrutiny.

"Tell you what," Willie offered. "Let me take a look and see what's wrong and what it will cost. Then we can talk. I won't charge you for checking it out."

"Oh, thank you!"

Rachel tried not to gush her gratitude, but she felt an immense load off her shoulders. If she knew what to expect, she felt she could handle it better.

Jesse gestured toward the diner.

"Would you like to join me for lunch? I was just on my way when your dog persuaded me to come help you. By the way, my name is Jesse Williams."

Rachel wasn't sure she was ready to be friendly with this guy. His abrasive manner when her truck was stalled behind his still grated on her. She started to decline when her stomach growled – loudly. She tried to disregard the gurgling sounds from her traitorous middle as she backed away from him.

"No, thanks. I'm sorry Angel kept you from your lunch. You go ahead. I think I'll just look around the town."

She hesitated, then looked up at him and offered a small smile.

"Thanks for your help. I'm sorry my "rust bucket" got in your way today."

Rachel called her dog to her and started to walk away from the men. Angel moved in front of her and gave her "the look."

"Come on, Angel," Rachel muttered. "Don't do this again."

Jesse laughed.

"I think your angel wants you to go eat. Maybe she's hoping for a doggy bag."

He took Rachel's elbow, giving her a surprised look when she stiffened slightly and pulled away from him. He stepped away from her and motioned toward the diner.

"Come on, it will be my treat. Angel can hang out in the back of my truck."

Jesse thought about David and Christy waiting for him at Mary Ann's. They knew people all over this area. Maybe they could help this prickly young woman find a job. It was worth a try.

"Come on. Mary Ann's Diner has some of the best food I ever ate. Besides, I have some friends I want you to meet. I think they'll be very helpful for you."

Rachel looked at him hopefully, the tension she had felt when he touched her arm easing.

"Do you think they might know where I could get a job?"

"Well, I don't want to promise anything. But they know a lot of people."

The aromas of fried chicken and coffee teased Rachel's senses as she and Jesse entered the old-fashioned diner. Small tables were scattered in the center of the room, with booths lining the walls near the street. A long counter with stools stretched across the far side of the room. Behind the counter waitresses and cook staff bustled around feeding the hungry lunch crowd.

Jesse motioned toward a table near the back where an older couple sat. They looked up from their coffee cups and waved at him.

Rachel smiled shyly as Jesse introduced her to David

and Christy Michaels. She was pleasantly surprised when Jesse held her chair for her when she sat down. While the three chatted for a moment, Rachel took the time to study the couple. David and Christy looked like they were in their 50's, but still seemed active and fit. David's brown hair was tinged with silver and slightly thinner on top. Christy's brown eyes sparkled with fun and were a perfect complement to her shoulder length silver-blond hair.

"Rachel, Jesse tells us you're new in town. Are you planning to stay or just passing through?"

"I'm not sure yet. I guess that depends on what's wrong with my truck and how much I'll have to earn to pay for it. I like small towns and I think I would like to stay here, for a while at least. Do you know of any jobs around here? I'm a good cook and housekeeper. I can take care of children or animals. I can learn quickly."

Rachel stopped, realizing she was beginning to sound desperate. Well, she *was* desperate. Her funds were almost gone and her truck was out of commission.

The waitress came up just then to take their order. When Rachel hesitated, Jesse gave her an encouraging nod. She ordered a hamburger and fries with a large soft drink. The others gave their orders, then looked over at Rachel after the waitress left.

"I think I know someone that could use your services, Rachel," David commented. "In fact, Jesse, I'm surprised you didn't think of it first. Jesse's employer, Kendall Ford, owns a ranch a few miles outside of town. The lady who did her cleaning and cooking just moved to Georgia to take care of her mother. Kendall's been at her wit's end trying to manage the ranch and her household."

Jesse cringed inwardly. He knew Kendall was having a hard time. She preferred ranch work over housework and didn't mind telling others that fact. But he wasn't sure he wanted this stranger cooking their food. Rachel seemed sweet and polite, and even kind of pretty. However, there was something almost furtive about the way she acted. As if she was running away or hiding. Jesse didn't mind helping with her junky truck or buying her lunch, but having her live at the same ranch with him?

"So, what do you think, Jesse? Rachel can stay with us tonight, then we'll bring her to the ranch tomorrow."

"Huh?"

Jesse realized they had been planning while his mind wandered. They were actually planning to take this complete stranger into their home. While he tried to think of a reason they shouldn't do that, Rachel offered her own.

"I don't want to impose on you. We just met. You don't know anything about me, and, quite frankly, I don't know anything about you. Also, I have a dog. She needs to stay with me."

David and Christy nodded their understanding of her objection, then began to explain why she should stay with them anyway. They always helped visitors to their town. They loved dogs and would be happy to have Angel come with her. And, where else would she sleep, since her truck was in the shop and she couldn't afford a motel room?

Rachel watched Jesse out of the corner of her eye. She could see he was not happy with the idea of her staying and working at the ranch where he worked. Her ire began to rise. Who did he think he was, anyway? Just because he had a better truck and could afford to buy her lunch, did he think he was better than she was? Rachel determined she would pay for her own lunch, even if it took her last penny. She turned to the sweet couple offering her shelter and accepted.

"Well, I guess I have to throw myself on your mercy," she laughed. "At least until I can get a job and pay my own way."

She hesitated a moment.

"Would you allow me to help with your housework or cooking as a thank you?"

Rachel knew some women preferred to control their own household and kitchen. She didn't want to offend or hurt anyone's feelings.

Christy smiled.

"We'll see. First, why don't you and Jesse go after lunch and get your things from your truck. Talk with Willie to find out what it's going to cost to get it fixed. Then you can get your dog and come on home with us. Jesse, can you let Kendall know we'll be bringing Rachel out tomorrow morning to meet her?"

Jesse took a moment to answer.

"Yeah, I'll tell her."

He ate his lunch in silence as Christy chatted with Rachel. David threw in a word or two now and then. It seemed that the three of them were getting along famously. Jesse didn't know why, but he felt put out that they became so friendly so quickly. He thought the Michaels were getting awfully chummy with a complete stranger.

"Jesse, you're awfully quiet."

Christy tried to bring him into the conversation, but he just gave her a brief smile, then waved for the waitress to bring the ticket. Rachel began rummaging in her purse, but felt a hand on her arm. She looked up to see Christy's sweet smile.

"Don't worry about that, this time," Christy told her. "Lunch is on David and me. You and Jesse go ahead."

Jesse started to object, but David shook his head.

"Don't even try it, Jesse. You know you'll lose that argument. Just do what my wife says and we'll all get along just fine."

Rachel got up from her chair before Jesse could come around to help her. She was still angry that he didn't seem to want her here. Or maybe he didn't want her working at the same place he worked. Well, he would have to just get over it. Rachel needed a job, and if this Kendall Ford would hire her, she would take that job.

Jesse started to touch her elbow again, then decided against it. He could see a spark in her eyes that meant she was angry with him, even though he had no idea what she had to be angry about. Hadn't he helped her get her rust bucket to the service station and invited her to lunch? The woman was just ungrateful after everything he had done for her.

The pair stalked across the street, not even looking at each other. Willie's eyes widened when he saw them approaching. He pulled out a grease rag and wiped his hands before stepping up to address Rachel.

"Well, young lady, I'm afraid it's bad news. Your engine is shot, the transmission is in almost as bad a shape, and the steering is barely hanging on. I can fix it, but it will cost a bundle. Is it worth it to you?"

Rachel fought back tears. There was no way she could afford all those repairs.

Jesse laughed.

"If you ask me, it seems like the best thing you could do for that old piece of junk is bury it."

Rachel wheeled on him; her hands clenched into fists. She started to raise one, but slowly returned it to her side.

"I didn't ask you!" she snapped. She turned back to Willie.

"What if we got used parts? Would that save some money?"

Willie considered for a moment.

"Possibly, but there's still a charge for labor. That's going to be a lot of work. And you still don't have a way to pay for it."

Now Rachel was getting desperate. Then she had an idea.

"Could you just park the truck at the back of your lot for a little while? I can pay a little bit for rent for the spot. I think I might be getting a job tomorrow, then we can work something out."

The mechanic looked down for a moment, as if pondering a heavy question, then looked back up at her with a grin.

"I never could resist a pretty girl in trouble. Sure, I'll put the truck in the back corner. Don't worry about rent. I never use that spot anyway. I got a friend in Shreveport that owns a junkyard. Maybe he can find what you need."

Jesse snorted. "That's about right for that truck."

He looked over at Rachel and bit off any further comments. It wasn't the anger that had been there before that stopped him. It was the tears that stood in her eyes now. He began to feel like a jerk for the way he had talked to her. Aunt Abigail would have his hide if she knew he had talked to a young woman like that. He was ashamed of himself, but his pride wouldn't let him admit it.

"Come on," he told her shortly. "Get your stuff and we'll go see if your dog is still in my truck or is trying to herd someone else."

He stopped and thought for a moment, then softened his expression.

"Welcome to Forrestville."

Chapter Five

Rachel gazed in wonder at the pastures and barns as David drove through the gate and down the long winding driveway. Above the gate was a metal sign that had a "K" with a rocker under it. She could see horses trotting in one pasture; their sleek coats gleaming in the sunshine. Cows grazed in a pasture further away. Angel sat next to her in the back seat. Rachel could see the dog's eyes trained on the cattle and the cowhands that worked with them.

"This is it."

David parked the car and came around to open the doors for Christy and Rachel. The old-fashioned courtesy in the gesture impressed Rachel. She had not been on the receiving end of such gallantry until Jesse had pulled her chair out the day before.

"Welcome to the Rocking K."

A tall woman in her forties, wearing jeans, boots, and a cowboy hat walked up to them and offered her hand.

"I'm Kendall Ford. Jesse told me you were coming."

She turned to Rachel with a smile.

"He told me you wanted to apply for the job as a housekeeper and cook at the ranch. Tell me about yourself and what kind of experience you have in cooking for large groups and cleaning large houses."

Rachel nodded and gave a detailed description of her experience with Marcus Taylor. She described the dinner parties she had cooked for and her duties cleaning his house and the cottages on the estate.

"In addition to working for Mr. Taylor, I cooked and kept house for my father, until he died a little over a year ago."

She almost choked on the last few words and looked down until she could control the tears that threatened. Rachel took a deep breath, then looked back at the group. Their sympathetic expressions almost caused her to lose her battle against the sadness, but she managed to hold it together and even offered a smile.

"So, you can see that I have experience cooking for both large and small groups. I can provide you with a resumé and references if you want."

As she said the words, Rachel realized she was in trouble if Kendall wanted a reference. Her only job had been working for the man whose nephew she had killed.

Kendall waved away the idea of a resumé.

"I prefer to talk with the people I'm looking to hire. Paperwork is just something else to keep up with. That's why I have an accountant. I believe I can tell more about a person by having an honest face-to-face talk."

Rachel remembered one of her most popular skills.

"I also enjoy baking and making desserts."

At that, the ranch owner grinned widely.

"That right there gets you hired, young lady. I have an enormous sweet tooth and quite a few of the hands do too. We'll be happy to have someone who can satisfy that. Come on in the house and we'll work out your salary. You can live in one of the cabins on the ranch. Each one has one bedroom, one bath, a small living room, and a kitchenette."

Rachel was overjoyed. She had a job! Then she looked down at Angel, who was still watching the cattle and cowhands.

"Oh!" she exclaimed. "I forgot about Angel. Can she stay with me? She's a good dog and never causes any trouble."

Kendall looked at the Border Collie with a troubled expression. She tapped her bottom lip with her finger.

"I don't know," she answered. "We usually only allow working animals on the ranch. We don't generally keep pets."

Rachel was in a quandary. She needed the job, but what could she do with Angel? The dog had saved her life. She couldn't just abandon her.

She sighed and was about to decline the job when there was a commotion at the nearby pasture. The hands were yelling about a calf that had broken free and was headed for the road.

Angel took off, running straight for the wayward animal. She got around in front of it and barked. The calf changed direction, still running. Angel continued to herd, getting in front and barking, or running alongside, until the calf returned to the corral.

The group in the driveway and the cowhands in the pasture stopped to stare while the dog herded the calf back where it belonged. The cowhands pointed at Rachel and Angel, calling out questions.

Kendall waved them off and turned back to Rachel, staring thoughtfully at her, then at the dog. She motioned to one of the cowhands, an older man with leathery skin, deep creases around his eyes, and a kindly smile. When he trotted over, she introduced him to the group.

"Hey, Spence, didn't you tell me there was a dog like this that went missing about six months ago?"

The cowhand pondered the question for a moment, letting his eyes rest on Angel as she sat near the corral, watching the calf she had herded. His eyes brightened.

"That's right! Old man Kershaw had a Border Collie. She was a young dog, but real smart. She could herd cattle like nobody's business. His heart started to give out a year or so ago, so he had to get rid of the herd. She stuck right with him, though."

Rachel felt a sinking in her heart. Did her dog belong to someone else? If so, how did she wind up at that rest stop?

Kendall nodded.

"I remember you told me about Mr. Kershaw dying. Whatever happened to his dog?"

"Well, there wasn't anyone to take her. He didn't have any family and he didn't have a will to tell what he wanted done with his stuff. None of the other farms or ranches around here asked for her. Then, one day, she just took off."

Rachel was afraid to ask, but had to know.

"Do you think my Angel is that dog?"

Spence looked at her and winked.

"Can't rightly say, young lady. But, don't seem to matter. She's your dog now."

"I tell you what," Kendall offered. "If you let that dog work with my hands during the day, she can stay with you at night. I can use a good herding dog like that."

Rachel called Angel back to her. The Border Collie trotted back, the expression on her face one of pure joy and satisfaction. Rachel fought tears again as she rubbed her head and told her what a good girl she was. She was so relieved that she could keep Angel.

Kendall offered her hand for the dog to smell, then scratched her behind the ears. Angel soaked up the attention, her tail wagging furiously.

While David and Christy chatted with Kendall, Rachel walked to their SUV to get her things. She gathered up Angel's supplies and put some of them in a shopping bag, which she handed to the dog to carry. Kendall grinned when she saw the little dog carrying her stuff.

"That's what I like to see," she approved. "Everyone doing their fair share."

After hugging David and Christy and thanking them for their help, Rachel followed Kendall into the main house. Built in a log cabin design, it had a rugged, cozy feel to it. Rachel liked the large family room with couches and chairs arranged in front of a huge fireplace. Since it was early summer, there was no fire in it, but she could picture it in the winter with logs blazing and people gathered around with mugs of cocoa in their hands. Rachel wondered if she would still be here then.

When she walked into the kitchen, however, she had to stop and catch her breath. It was furnished with everything a cook could possibly want. Two large refrigerators, a six-burner stove, a kitchen island for washing, chopping, and prepping. Rachel thought she could happily work in here for hours.

After touring the house, Kendall led Rachel out the back door in the kitchen to see the barn, stables, and cabins. She pointed to the first of a row of small cabins and told Rachel that one would be hers. It wasn't fancy, but it looked solid and neat.

"Kendall!"

One of the hands ran up. When he got closer, Rachel saw it was Jesse Williams. Now he was hot and sweaty, his face red from exertion.

"The new cow is in labor!"

"Now?"

Kendall shook her head in disbelief.

"She's early. I better call Doctor Gray."

"I already did. She's on the way."

Kendall clapped him on the back.

"Thanks, Jesse. I don't know what I'd do without you."

Rachel didn't know it was possible for his face to get any redder, but it did. She wondered if he was embarrassed by Kendall praising him in front of her. Somehow it seemed endearing.

"Jesse, have you met Rachel? She's our new cook and housekeeper."

He gave Rachel a cool, indifferent glance; as if she was of no importance at all. Rachel felt her temper rise. So, he still thought he was better than her, huh? She had to bring her attention back to Kendall who was still speaking.

"Jesse is one of my best men. In fact, he's just about become my right-hand man, right after Spence. And that's going some since Spence has been with me for about fifteen years."

Rachel gave Jesse a frosty stare. If he wanted to be cold with her, she would reciprocate the sentiment.

"I met Mr. Williams in town yesterday when my truck died behind his."

She realized she was acting rather ungrateful after the way he had helped her the day before. But his attitude still rankled.

"He helped me push my truck to Willie's. Then he showed me to the diner and introduced me to the Michaels."

Kendall nodded approvingly.

"That's Jesse. Helping everyone. Listen, Jess, I need your help now."

"With the cow in labor?"

Jesse really hoped she wasn't about to ask him what he was afraid she was going to ask. But his hope was in vain.

"No, Doctor Gray will help with the cow. But I need to be there. Would you finish showing Rachel around? All I've shown her so far is the house. Would you show her the barn, stables, and just around this area? You don't need to go out to the pastures or anything like that. Just the immediate area."

Before Jesse could object Kendall turned to Rachel.

"I know I'm leaving you in good hands, Rachel. Jesse will show you around. After the tour, just grab your stuff from the house to put in your cabin. It should be stocked with towels and linens, but if you need anything, you can get it from the main house."

With that the ranch owner hurried toward the barn just in time to meet the veterinarian who was pulling her truck into the parking area near the barn.

Jesse and Rachel stood in stony silence for a moment. Finally, Rachel lifted her head and gave him a defiant look.

"I know you don't want me here," she said. "Although I don't know why. But I *need* this job. So I'm staying."

Jesse had the grace to look ashamed.

"I'm sorry I made you feel unwelcome," he muttered. "I guess I just wasn't comfortable with a complete stranger coming in here."

When he saw her about to object, he hurried to continue.

"But, hey, I was a complete stranger when I came, so, well, anyway."

He breathed out a sigh of frustration.

"Come on and let me show you around. The Rocking K is a great place. I think you and Angel will like it here."

Rachel took in a long breath as she looked around. She watched her dog already working with some of the hands. She saw two foals racing each other around one of the pastures. Then she looked at Jesse and smiled.

"I think I will too."

"This is the stables."

Jesse had saved what he considered to be the best for last. He loved coming into the stables. The combined smells of wood, hay, leather, and horses were soothing for him. This was where he came when he needed to unwind.

He watched Rachel as she stood in the doorway, taking it all in. Her expressive face registered awe at the space. He could understand. When he first came to the Rocking K, Jesse had been amazed at the way Kendall had everything possible to keep her horses in tip-top shape.

"Wow! It looks like Kendall thought of everything for these horses!" Rachel echoed Jesse's thoughts.

"I think I could sleep in here and be as comfortable as in my little cabin," she laughed.

Jesse decided he liked this side of Rachel. As they toured the ranch, she had relaxed and seemed to be enjoying seeing everything on the ranch. He could see she loved the horses, as she walked down the aisle and stopped to stroke a nose or murmur a few words.

Jesse's muscles tightened when Rachel stopped in front of a huge brown stallion. The horse snorted when she approached the stall, and danced a few steps away. Rachel stood still and spoke soothingly to the nervous stallion. He watched as she looked at the name plate on the stall, then called the animal by his name, Thunder, in a soft voice. Just when it seemed the horse was calming down and responding to Rachel, he laid his ears back and snorted angrily again.

"That's my horse."

They turned and saw a young man in his twenties with short brown hair and intense green eyes. Jesse knew the cowhand was someone who had arrived at the ranch within the past few months, having been arrested multiple times for a long string of barroom fights.

"Rachel, this is Jason. He's fairly new to the ranch. Jason, this Rachel, our new cook."

Jason barely inclined his head as he stared past Rachel at the stallion behind her.

"Kendall said I can break and train that horse, so I don't want anyone around him until I do."

Rachel wasn't quite sure what to think of the young cowhand. He was rude, certainly. He also seemed arrogant, thinking he could order people to stay away from a horse their employer owned. She decided to try a little diplomacy.

"I guess you're pretty excited to get to break and train a beautiful animal like Thunder. Do you have a lot of experience with horses?"

Jesse barely kept from snorting in derision. He answered her before Jason could open his mouth.

"Jason just came to the ranch six months ago. Before that he lived in Shreveport."

He glanced at Jason.

"You lived in the city, didn't you, Jason? Not around horses much."

Jason glared at him.

"I've had some experiences with horses," he retorted. "Why don't you pay attention to your own business and stay out of mine."

He turned his attention to Rachel.

"Just remember what I said and stay away from my horse."

Jason stalked out of the stable.

"Don't pay him any attention."

Jesse and Rachel turned at the sound of Kendall's voice. She was standing in the door at the other end of the stable.

"I told Jason he could help Spence with breaking and training Thunder, but that does not make the stallion his. You are free to go anywhere on the property and visit any of the animals you want to visit. I do want to caution you, though. Thunder came to us from our police chief. She rescued him from a guy who was abusing him. He's pretty nervous around people and gets agitated very easily. So, be careful. I don't want anyone getting hurt here."

As if to confirm her words, the huge stallion snorted and danced around his stall again. Kendall motioned for Jesse and Rachel to follow her.

"Let's give him some peace and quiet. That will help him settle down. Rachel, do you feel up to starting tonight? Or would you rather rest and start fresh with breakfast tomorrow?"

Rachel's face lit up.

"Oh, I'd love to start tonight. Let me get in the kitchen and see what I can find."

Kendall nodded, her smile showing approval.

"I was hoping you would say that. Let's go. I can't wait to see how good my new cook is."

Jesse wouldn't admit it, but he was looking forward to trying Rachel's cooking too. She was starting to grow on him.

Chapter Six

Rachel hummed quietly as she gave a final swipe to the already clean table. After three weeks at the Rocking K, she was beginning to relax. She loved her job cooking for Kendall and the cowhands. They were great fans of her breads and casseroles. When she fixed spaghetti for them, they cheered. But their highest praise was reserved for her desserts. Whether it was chocolate cake, banana pudding, or fudge brownies, the entire crew devoured the sweets. It made Rachel feel good to know she was a contributing member of the Rocking K family.

She hung up the kitchen towel and glanced at the clock. It was only 2:00, so she had time to take a walk. Rachel wanted to see how Angel was doing. Each night, after dinner, she found her dog either sitting or laying in front of their cabin, waiting patiently for her. When she let herself and the collie in, Rachel filled the water and food bowls. Angel would eat, then plop down on her bed. The dog seemed very content with her life at the ranch.

Rachel also wanted to visit the stables and get another look at Thunder. Spence and Jason had been working with the big horse. Spence was careful and patient with the abused animal, but Jason tended to have a heavy hand with him.

Spence spent as much time correcting Jason as he did training the horse. Thunder made it clear he did not like the young cowhand.

The stallion always snorted and either reared or pulled away whenever Jason came around him. No matter what the young cowhand did, the horse wanted nothing to do with him.

Thunder did, however, seem to like Rachel. Whenever she came near his stall and spoke softly to him, the stallion would calm, his large brown eyes watching her.

Jason had expressed his disdain for Rachel's ability to settle Thunder. He still insisted that he was training Thunder and that Rachel should leave the horse alone; often his voice and words became almost threatening.

He made sure Kendall and Spence were nowhere around when he tried to intimidate Rachel. She had managed to keep her temper so far, but she was about fed up with his attempts at bullying her.

The stables felt cool after the walk in the June heat. Rachel pulled a piece of apple from her pocket and offered it to Thunder. He gave a soft nicker as he took the fruit, his velvety lips tickling her hand.

Rachel sensed Jason's presence right before he grabbed her shoulder and pulled her around to face him.

"I told you to leave my horse alone!"

His heavy brows pulled into a frown on his red face.

"Kendall told me I could go anywhere I wanted on this property," she reminded him. Rachel didn't want to get into a fight with Jason, but she would not back down if he started one.

"You don't have Kendall or the old man to help you," he taunted her. "I don't care how pretty you are; I'm going to kick your . . ."

Jason's words cut off as Rachel's hand whipped out and grabbed his wrist. She quickly whirled him around with his arm behind him.

"My what?"

He struggled for a moment, then went still. Rachel's grip relaxed, thinking the young bully had learned not to mess with her. Suddenly he whipped around with his hand raised to slap her.

Rachel's arm went up instinctively to block the blow as the other hand delivered a blow to his ribs. Jason cursed at her as he doubled over in pain. She stepped back and watched him warily. At this point she didn't want to turn her back on him to leave. Rachel would not be fooled into relaxing her guard again.

By now several cowhands had drifted into the stables and were standing around watching them. One or two had thought to rescue Rachel at first, but when they saw her reaction to Jason's attempt to strike her, they decided she didn't need their help. One of them, however, ran to get Kendall. Jesse came in and looked around to see what the ruckus was. When he saw Jason and Rachel facing off, he surged forward. Spence grabbed him.

"Hold on there, buddy. That little lady don't need your help. She's handling him just fine herself."

It was true. Every time Jason moved to strike Rachel, she countered him. Finally he just charged her, as if to back her into a corner.

By now Rachel was moving automatically; her years of self-defense training providing the moves without conscious thought. When the bully charged her, Rachel had had enough. She sidestepped him, then wrapped her arm around his neck and began to apply pressure. Jason's struggles began to falter.

With a jolt Rachel came to herself and realized what she was doing. Horrified, she dropped her arm from around her victim's neck and watched him stagger to a nearby bale of hay. A sob erupted as she turned and fled from the stable, pushing through the crowd.

Kendall was standing by Thunder's stall, soothing the horse as he snorted and reared at the sight of the would-be trainer. She watched as her new cook put the hot-headed cowhand in a choke-hold, then release him and run away in tears. Kendall caught Jesse's eye and motioned for him to follow Rachel and make sure she was okay. Jesse nodded and headed in that direction.

"Jason, come with me."

Kendall was calm, but her voice was steely.

"Did you see what she did to me?" he whined. "She almost choked me."

"I saw a lot more than you realize," she replied. "We can discuss it here or in my office."

"I don't need to go your office," he blustered. "Say what you want to say in front of the guys. I got nothin' to hide."

Kendall nodded.

"Very well. You will not be training Thunder any longer. I have fence line in the south pasture that needs to be repaired."

"But . . ." he started.

She held up her hand.

"No argument. You can take off the rest of today. Tomorrow morning after breakfast you'll head out to the south pasture. Don't forget your gloves and water. You'll need them."

When Kendall saw that Jason was about to lose his temper, she reminded him, "You will do as I say or you can return to the jail in Shreveport. It's your choice."

Jason glared at her for a moment, then looked down and nodded.

"Yes, ma'am," he muttered. He stalked off to his cabin, rubbing his tender neck and wishing he had never seen that horse or that pretty young cook.

Jesse found Rachel in the kitchen, sobbing into a dishtowel. When she looked up at him, he opened his arms and she stepped into his comforting embrace. He didn't say anything at first, just wrapped his arms around her and held her. When Rachel's tears seemed to slow, he set her back and looked her over carefully.

"Did he hurt you?"

Jesse's voice indicated that if the bully had left so much as a scratch on Rachel, he would find the man and beat him to a pulp.

Rachel shook her head.

"No," she choked out. "He didn't lay a hand on me."

Jesse was puzzled. If she wasn't hurt, why was she crying?

"Rachel, I don't understand. Why are you so upset? Are you afraid of Jason? You seemed to handle him, and yourself, very well in the stable."

Rachel's eyes filled with tears again, but she wiped them away with the soggy dishtowel that she still held twisted in her hands.

"Jesse."

She stopped and tried to get the words out without bursting into sobs again.

"Jesse, I could have killed him. Just like Co . . I could have killed him without even . . . I'm not scared of him. I'm scared of myself! I'm scared of what I almost did just now!"

Jesse's eyes narrowed.

"You started to say a name. Just like, who?"

Rachel averted her gaze, staring at the dishtowel as if it held all the answers. Jesse reached over and took the towel from her. He lifted her chin with gentle fingers.

"Talk to me. Who did you fight? Who did you kill?"

Jesse was being as gentle as he knew how, but his chest hurt. Had he been taken in by a pretty face who was actually a killer? He shook the thought away. No way. Rachel was a gentle soul. She could not have killed anyone; at least, not on purpose.

He thought about the skill Rachel showed as she fought Jason. She certainly had the knowledge and ability. Jesse looked deep into her eyes.

Rachel's face contorted with grief. She wrenched away from him and went to stand by the kitchen island, her shoulders heaving as she sobbed. Finally, she turned back to face Jesse.

"I used to live in Austin," she began. "My employer's nephew, Colin Taylor, was always trying to flirt with me; touching my hand or my shoulder. Sometimes he would stand really close."

"I had my own little cottage to live in. One day I got home and found him waiting in my cottage. He was drunk."

Rachel stopped and shuddered. She could still remember Colin's drunken grin and slurred words.

"He, he tried to, he tried to r..rape me. I was in panic mode. I didn't even think, I just reacted. When I came to myself, he was laying on the floor. He was completely limp."

She looked up at Jesse with horror in her eyes.

"Jesse, I killed him! I killed a man! I was so scared that I just packed my stuff and left."

"You didn't call the police?"

Jesse tried to grasp what she just told him. His stomach churned when he thought about the man trying to rape this sweet, gentle girl. As far as Jesse was concerned the guy got what was coming to him.

"No, I didn't call the police! Don't you understand? I had just killed the nephew, and probably the heir, of a wealthy and influential man. Do you think they would have believed I was just defending myself?"

Rachel was bordering on hysteria now. Jesse reached out and drew her to him for another hug, gently rubbing her back until her sobs quieted and her breathing returned to normal. She pulled back and scrubbed her eyes and cheeks.

"Are you going to turn me in?"

Fear glimmered in her eyes.

Jesse shook his head.

"No, I think that's something for you to do when you're ready. But, Rachel,"

He captured her gaze again to make sure she was listening.

"I don't think you murdered him. From what you've told me, it was pure self-defense."

"But do you see why I'm afraid of myself? Of what I could do?"

"Yeah, I get it."

He had watched his friend Esther in the martial arts school where she taught. Esther was highly skilled and had incredible control of her movements. Rachel had the skill, but was afraid she didn't have the control.

"It's okay."

He took her hand and rubbed the back of it in soothing circles.

"I think I understand. You're afraid you don't have the control you need, right?"

Rachel nodded. She had always struggled with control. Uncle Jon had admonished her about that throughout the years he trained her.

"Skill without control is dangerous. You have to develop both."

"I'm scared that if I feel I'm in danger, I could seriously hurt or kill someone again," she admitted.

Jesse stood without commenting, his mind working on a solution. When one came to him, he grinned.

"I have a friend who teaches martial arts, Esther Abrams. She's really good and has great control. I bet she could help you."

Rachel started to shake her head, but as she mulled over his words, she realized he might have a good idea. Maybe getting someone to help her learn control would help. She could ask Esther to help her focus more on the control issue than on learning moves.

"Is her class expensive?"

Rachel was trying to keep her spending to a bare minimum so that she could send as much as possible to help pay for Uncle Jon's rehab.

She saw Jesse looking at her strangely and realized he was wondering why she would worry about the cost of the classes when most of her needs were met at the ranch.

"My father and uncle were in an awful car wreck a little over a year ago. Dad died and Uncle Jon was badly injured. He's been in a rehab facility for the past several months. Most of my check goes to pay for his care."

"I'm sorry about you losing your father, Rachel. I remember how bad I felt when my mom died. It's great that you're helping your uncle. But, you know, if he wanted you to learn control, he would probably want you to let Esther help you."

Rachel had to agree. Uncle Jon would probably tell her to jump at the chance to learn something she had long struggled with.

"Okay," she conceded. "Will you give me directions to her dojo?"

Jesse squeezed her hand.

"I'll do better than that. I'll take you there myself."

Rachel closed the screen door behind her, being careful to not let it slam shut. She turned to scan the yard, then beyond that to the stables and pastures. Rachel never tired of the view from the house. The green pastures with cows grazing and the training yard with the horses trotting and walking always gave her a feeling of peace.

Peace, she wondered. Was there a peace that was always present, not just in these fleeting moments? Daddy and Uncle Jon believed that God gave them His peace when He forgave them.

Rachel shuddered. How could God forgive her? She had killed a man. It was in self-defense, she argued with herself. She did what she had to do to protect herself. But Rachel had grown up learning the Ten Commandments and she knew one of them said, "Do not kill."

As far as she could see it, she had blown any chance for forgiveness or peace. She just had to enjoy the little moments of peace that came her way and make the most of those.

Shaking her head to dispel the disturbing thoughts, Rachel looked around to see if she could find Jesse. Since her fight with Jason a few weeks prior, she and Jesse had begun to seek each other out for talks. Sometimes the talks were serious. Sometimes they just chatted about their day or happenings around the ranch. He was someone she could talk to and was comfortable around. There were no demands on her in Jesse's presence.

Rachel wondered if Jesse had the peace she longed for. She had seen him going to church with Kendall and a few of the other cowhands. Kendall had invited her to go with them, but Rachel had declined. She was afraid God would strike her down if she dared enter a church with the sin of murder on her soul.

But Jesse not only went to church, he was actively involved. It seemed whenever he had a spare moment, he was off to help with something at church or in the community.

Jesse was standing near the paddock stroking on Thunder's neck. Spence had gotten the horse comfortable with being around people. However, the stallion seemed to prefer Jesse and Rachel, often trotting up to one of them when they came near the paddock or the stables, nosing their hands or pockets in search of a treat. Since Jason was not allowed around the Thunder, the horse had calmed considerably.

Rachel stopped a few feet short and admired the picture Jesse and Thunder made. Jesse wasn't movie-star handsome, but his curly dark hair and intense brown eyes drew her in. He was someone Rachel could see herself becoming attracted to – if she wasn't a fugitive from the law.

"Jesse,"

Rachel spoke softly so she would not startle the horse. When Jesse turned to look at her, Rachel walked up to stand in front of him.

"I just heard from Willie," she told him. "He says my truck is ready for me to come get it. He finally got it running."

"That's good."

Jesse grinned impishly.

"It's great that he got it running. Will that old rust bucket stop when it's supposed to?"

Rachel's cheeks reddened and her eyes snapped. The one thing Jesse did that always got her riled up was put down her faithful little truck. He just didn't understand her connection with it. She had travelled over 300 miles in that little truck and it was like an old friend to her.

"Yes, it will stop," she snapped at him. "Willie said it's good as new."

Jesse looked like he wanted to make another snarky remark, but Kendall walked up with a list in hand, just before he said something else to aggravate Rachel.

"Jesse, I sure appreciate your picking these things up for me. When you're done, go have lunch at the diner. Tell them to put it on the ranch's tab."

"Can I ride in with you?"

Rachel had almost decided to wait and ride with someone else after Jesse gave her a hard time about her truck, but she really needed to go to town and pay for the repairs. She also needed her own transportation so she wouldn't have to ask for rides all the time.

Jesse gave her an impish grin and waved his hand toward his own pickup.

"Please join me for a ride to town in my comfortable, air-conditioned chariot. Notice that it runs smoothly and stops when I push the brake pedal."

Rachel was tempted to put him in a head lock just for a minute, then decided it was in her best interest to seem to ignore the comment. She gave him a sweet smile.

"While we're in town, maybe you can point out Esther's dojo. I want to meet her and see how much her classes are."

Jesse held the truck door open for her, then closed it once she was seated in the truck.

"Sure," he replied. "I'd be glad to."

"Do you know martial arts?" Rachel asked him innocently. "Have you ever taken classes at the dojo?"

She knew he had not, she was just reminding him what she was capable of doing. Jesse shot her an annoyed look as he started the truck. He had gotten the message.

"Here you go, missy. Sorry it took so long, but some of those parts were hard to find."

Rachel shook her head.

"I'm just grateful you were able to fix my little truck. How much do I owe you?"

When Willie handed her the bill, her eyes widened at the final cost.

"Willie, this amount is awfully low. Are you sure that's all I owe? I feel like I should pay you more for all the work you did."

"Young lady, that is the price. There is no negotiating once I do the work and give you the bill."

Rachel accepted the keys with tears in her eyes and gave the mechanic a spontaneous hug. He patted her on the back and stepped back, nervously wiping his hands on a shop rag. His face was red, but he looked pleased at her show of affection.

"Thank you for letting me serve you," he managed to choke out. Then he turned away and headed back to the service bays. When Rachel called out another thank you, he just waved and kept going.

Rachel turned to find Jesse watching with surprise.

"What?"

He shook his head.

"You just didn't seem the hugging type."

Rachel smiled.

"You think you have me pegged, huh? Well, just watch and see. I might have more surprises for you."

She finished her sentence by batting her eyes at him in an exaggerated flirting expression. Then she caught herself. What was she doing flirting? Jesse was a friend; becoming a good friend. But she couldn't afford to let it go any further than that.

Rachel fidgeted with her keys, then climbed into her truck.

"So, where is that martial arts dojo?"

As Rachel entered the martial arts school, Jesse watched her stop at the edge of the mat and bow, as all students do when entering the dojo. Esther looked up from the student she was teaching and saw Rachel. After getting the student started on a series of moves, Esther came toward her. Rachel bowed and Esther returned the bow, then introduced herself.

Jesse hung back and watched the women. Though Rachel seemed shy most of the time, in the school she seemed to relax and open up.

"Hey, man, what are you doing here?"

Stephen Abrams, Esther's husband, clapped a hand on Jesse's shoulder.

"You ready to sign up for classes? Don't worry, we'll go easy on you."

Jesse just laughed at him. He was too busy to take on anything else, though he liked the idea of learning martial arts. All he knew was street fighting that he had learned from his time selling drugs. He preferred to forget about that time. Jesse worked hard at the ranch and wherever he was asked to serve in the hopes that the people of Forrestville would forget about that time also.

While he talked with Stephen, Jesse saw Esther's dog, Ninja, get up and trot toward the women. Rachel's look of delight warmed him inside. Her love of all animals was one of the things that attracted him.

Ninja sidled next to Rachel and nosed her hand until she stroked his back.

"What a beautiful dog!"

Esther beamed.

"Ninja was my brother Paul's K9 partner before Paul was killed in the line of duty. Ninja was shot at the same time and injured too severely to return to being a narcotics dog. Our police chief, Maggie, let me adopt him. He's pretty special to me."

"I can see why."

The two women stood petting the dog, while Ninja soaked up the attention. Jesse nudged Stephen and showed him the scene. The men laughed at the sight of the big dog and his admirers. Rachel and Esther looked up and saw them watching. They whispered together for a moment, then Esther waved them over.

The men joined the trio and Esther laid a hand on Rachel's shoulder.

"Stephen, this is Rachel James. She works at the Rocking K with Jesse and is interested in joining our dojo. Rachel already has martial arts training, but wants to work on control."

Esther grinned in anticipation.

"I can't wait to get her on the mat."

Jesse felt a nibble of worry inside. He hadn't thought about Esther being the one who would spar with Rachel. Since Esther was about half-way through her pregnancy, he thought she would have one of the other students do that part while Esther watched and gave instruction. Jesse didn't want Esther to get hurt trying to help Rachel with control issues.

"I'm fine, guys."

Esther rolled her eyes.

It was amazing how she knew what he was thinking. But then, he saw the worry on Stephen's face and realized his own expression probably mirrored it. Rachel laid her hand on Esther's arm.

"Sensei Esther, I really do have control issues."

Jesse appreciated Rachel's sensitivity to the situation, but he realized it was too late. Esther wasn't about to let Rachel get away now, not if Rachel showed the least bit of interest in studying at the dojo.

"Okay, all three of you listen to me."

Esther was exasperated now.

"I am pregnant, not dying. I am also an experienced martial arts instructor. I'm not going to put my baby or myself at risk. If I feel the situation calls for it, I will get one of the other senseis to take over. Satisfied?"

Stephen looked at his wife, then at Jesse and Rachel. They all nodded at each other. Esther shook her head at them and turned to Rachel.

"We have a class on Monday and Thursday evenings at 7:00. Will that time work for you? The classes last about two hours."

"I think I can handle that."

Jesse told Rachel to meet him at the diner after she finished working out the details, then left to pick up the items Kendall had asked him to get. He found he was beginning to enjoy any time he got to spend with Rachel. She was sweet and shy, but she also had a spark inside that he longed to watch to see if it would grow. He loved to watch her pretty, expressive face when she was talking with others and unaware of his eyes on her.

He snorted at himself. Why would this special young woman want to have anything to do with him? He was still on probation for selling drugs. No way she'd want to have anything more than a casual friendship with him.

Rachel hummed as she moved around the kitchen. The smell of chocolate filled the room, making her feel that scent was the best aromatherapy ever.

She checked the timer, then hurried to give the counter a final swipe with the sponge. Rachel tossed the sponge into the sink and grabbed a couple of potholders to arrange on the counter.

Just then she saw the swinging door between the kitchen and living room open a little and the top of a head poke through.

She sighed and shook her head, amused. Rachel had had three visitors already since she began preparing the favored dessert. She wondered who was checking the brownies' progress now.

Rachel was surprised to see Jason as he peered into the kitchen. A sliver of anxiety went through her. Was he going to cause trouble?

"Miss Rachel, can I come in?"

She nodded, quietly watching him.

He finished sidling through the door and just stood for a moment, his tanned and calloused hands fidgeting with his hat. Rachel was puzzled to see that there was no antagonism in his expression. In fact, he looked somewhat sheepish.

"Can I help you with something?"

Jason looked into her face briefly, then looked down. He cleared his throat, then looked up again.

"I came to apologize."

Wow! Rachel wasn't expecting that. Since the fight, Jason had not tried to approach her or talk to her. If their paths crossed, he did not say anything to her, or even look at her.

"Apologize for what?"

Rachel wasn't going to let him off easy. He needed to show that he was not going to harass or try to bully her again.

His face reddened, but he did not react angrily. In fact, he looked like he was going to cry. Rachel felt her heart begin to soften.

"I'm sorry I gave you such a hard time when you first came. Ms. Kendall talked with me and showed me it was wrong for me to treat you like that."

He gulped and turned his head away. Rachel could see this was not easy for him and was about to accept his apology when he turned back to her.

"I deserved the whupping you gave me. I even deserved the choke hold you put me in. If you don't mind, I'd like to call a truce."

Rachel smiled and held out her hand to him.

"Apology accepted. And I don't mind at all. I think a truce is a great idea."

Jason stared at her small hand for a second, then gave her a small smile as he shook with her.

"Truce."

Then he peeked around her at the oven.

"Are the brownies done yet?"

Chapter Seven

"Hey, Rachel, want to come to church with us?"

Kendall stuck her head around the doorway to the kitchen. When she saw Rachel with an apron on, getting a big bowl from the cabinet, she came in and firmly took hold of the bowl.

"No, ma'am, you do not work on Sunday. I think I've told you that before. Half-day on Saturday and all day Sunday is your time off. Come join us for church."

Rachel shook her head.

"No thanks, I have some things I need to do. I wasn't working, I was just going to try a recipe. Your kitchen is better for trying recipes."

Kendall eyed her suspiciously.

"Uh huh. And that recipe would just happen to turn into lunch, right? You know, you don't have to keep doing extra work. We love you here. Your job is quite secure."

"I know."

Rachel fidgeted with her apron, then sighed and took it off.

"I do have things to do at my cabin, so I guess I'll head over there."

She could feel Kendall watching her as she went out the back door.

Rachel went into her cabin and started puttering around, straightening up, dusting a little. She heard a knock at her door, then Jesse stuck his head in.

"Hey, Rachel! Want to come to church with us?"

Rachel had to smile when he said the same words that Kendall had used.

"No, thanks, Jesse. I have stuff I need to do here."

Jesse stepped into the cabin.

"What stuff?"

He looked around the small cabin.

"Your cabin looks nice and clean. I don't see anything that needs to be done. Come on with us."

Rachel glared at him.

"I said I have stuff to do. I don't need to answer to you or anyone else about what I do with my own time! And I don't recall inviting you into my cabin."

Jesse held his hands up in surrender, his face darkening at her hostile tone.

"Fine," he bit out. "Excuse me for intruding into your sacred space."

He turned and exited, closing the door a little more forcefully than needed.

Rachel sighed. She hated knowing she had been rude to Jesse, when he had been so nice to her since she came to work at the ranch. Their rough beginning in town had smoothed out and become a good friendship.

Her attraction to the young cowboy increased every day. His dark curly hair seemed to invite her to run her fingers through it. Sometimes she felt she could get lost in his intense dark eyes. But Rachel knew she could not give in to the attraction. It was for the same reason she could not go to church.

Her father had taken her to church when she was

young. She had even participated in some youth events. But when their finances took a downturn and Rachel had gone to work for Marcus Taylor, it became too easy to find reasons not to go to church.

The real reason, however, was that Rachel was afraid to go to church and face God there. She was afraid of Him and of His judgment. God couldn't forgive her for killing a man.

"Kendall, where's the remote? I need to get the TV set up."

"Just hold your horses, I'm coming. I had to find the DVD."

Kendall and several of the hands gathered in her living room. It was after dinner and they were settling in to watch a DVD of their church's recent revival service.

"Rachel, want to join us? Pastor Bill is really good."

"Oh, yeah!" one of the others chimed in. "I felt like I learned a lot from that sermon he preached the last night. Kendall, you had a good idea getting DVD's of the services."

Jesse looked over his shoulder and saw Rachel as she stood in the doorway watching the rain. It had been coming down for the past couple of hours and was expected to last until after midnight.

Rachel glanced into the living room, her gaze going straight to Jesse. She turned back to watching the weather outside.

"I might in a little while. I just wanted to get a look at the storm for a minute, then I need to finish up some things in the kitchen."

Jesse thought about objecting about her working so hard on Sunday, but he knew it was futile. Kendall had already talked to her about it. He plopped down on the couch next to Spence. Angel jumped up and laid her head in his lap. Jesse rubbed her head briefly, then made her get down. Kendall had allowed Angel in the house because of the storm, but did not allow animals on the furniture.

"So, is the little lady going to join us?"

Spence turned to try to see Rachel, but she had gone back into the kitchen.

"She said she might in a little while."

"Seems like that sweet girl is carrying some kind of a heavy load. Might do her some good to hear what this man has to say."

Jesse's heart was heavy as he agreed with Spence. Rachel was open and friendly most of the time, until someone suggested church or talked about God. Then, she became distant. Sometimes she became defensive and hostile, like the day he and Kendall invited her to go to church with them.

He turned his attention to the recorded service. The music was upbeat and the crowd in the living room sang along. Then the evangelist got up to preach. Soon the whole group was engrossed in the message and didn't notice when Rachel came to stand in the doorway.

"No matter what you have done," the preacher emphasized. "No matter what your sin, God can forgive you."

He came down from the stage to stand eye to eye with the audience.

"Let me repeat that. No matter what your sin, whatever you have done, God loves you. He is waiting for you to call on Him for forgiveness and cleansing."

"Is that true?"

Kendall and the others turned to see Rachel standing, trembling, with tears running down her face. Angel trotted around to stand next to Rachel, reaching up to lick her mistress' hand.

"Is what true, honey?"

Kendall got up and went to put an arm around her young housekeeper. Rachel had her arms wrapped around her stomach and was crying as she watched the evangelist as if he had just offered her a lifeline.

"Is it true that God can forgive anything I've done? That He loves me no matter what I've done?"

Jesse knew she was thinking about the man she had killed in self-defense. He knew it weighed her down, remembering she had taken someone's life. He got up and went to stand on the other side of Rachel. He took her hand and tugged her toward the kitchen.

"Come on, Rachel. Let's go talk about it."

Spence appeared behind Jesse and handed him his Bible, then gave Rachel a loving pat on the shoulder.

"You listen to this young man, missy. He's experienced this for himself and he can tell you how those words are true for him."

Rachel nodded and followed Jesse into the quiet kitchen. He sat at the breakfast bar and patted the stool next to him.

"You're thinking about the man you killed, aren't you?"

He kept his voice low as he looked Rachel in the eyes.

"How can God forgive that?"

Rachel swiped at the tears running down her cheeks.

"Doesn't the Bible say 'Thou shalt not murder?' I broke one of the commandments. How can God forgive that?"

Jesse thought for a moment. He wanted to point out that she didn't murder the man; she defended herself. But he knew that Rachel knew that herself. He turned in his Bible to a book near the back.

"Here, Rachel, I think this verse covers that. Let me read it. 'If we confess our sins, He is faithful and just to forgive us our sins, and to cleanse us from all unrighteousness.'"

He turned to face her.

"If we confess; that means we see the sin the way God does and we grieve about it like He does, then He forgives us. Not only that, He cleanses us. He washes our sin away."

Rachel stared transfixed at the words. After a moment Jesse turned to one of the gospels.

"You asked if He could forgive you for murder. Did you know that while they were crucifying Him, He forgave the very men who were killing Him and asked His Father to forgive them too? They were crucifying the Son of God and He forgave them while they were in the act of doing it!"

Jesse stopped when he realized he was talking loudly in his excitement. He lowered his voice again.

"Rachel, God knows that your sin has caused you a lot of grief, like a heavy weight you always carry. Would you like to confess that sin and receive His gift of forgiveness? Do you want to ask Jesus to cleanse you and save you?"

Rachel whispered, "Oh, yes! Yes I would! Will you help me?"

Jesse took her hand.

"I'll pray for you, then you tell God what's in your heart. Don't forget He sent His Son to pay for your forgiveness with His own life."

They both bowed their heads while Jesse prayed briefly for Rachel, as if he were introducing her to his loving Father. Rachel struggled for words for a moment, then began.

"Dear God, I need Your forgiveness. You know I killed that man in self-defense, but it still scares me. I know I have sinned in other ways too. I've tried to do things all by myself. I don't want to do that anymore. Please forgive me and save me. I accept Jesus as my Lord and Savior. Please cleanse me and lead me. Thank You God!"

"Amen!"

Jesse lifted his head and watched as Rachel dried her tears. He felt a sudden urge to take her in his arms and wipe those tears himself. Leading her to pray for salvation seemed to create a close, intimate bond between them. Rachel lifted a radiant smile to him.

"Thank you, Jesse." she bit her lip. "But, what do I do now?"

"What do you mean?"

"Well, isn't there more now?"

"You do need to grow. You are like a baby in Christ right now. Babies grow by feeding. Get you a good Bible and read it every day. Kendall can help you with that. She helped me pick out a good study Bible. You need to pray every day. Get to know your Heavenly Father. And you should go to church so you can be with other Christians. We help each other grow that way."

"Do I need to do some kind of work to keep God's forgiveness?"

Jesse was startled.

"Why would you think that?"

"Well, I see you working a lot. Besides what you do here, you're really busy at church and in the community. I see you doing things for others even when you're really tired."

Jesse knew she was right. He was still trying to prove to the community that he was not the man he used to be. And, he felt there might be something more to his constant need to work. That was something he wanted to think about later.

"No, Rachel, you do not have to work to keep God's forgiveness."

He took her hand and squeezed it.

"It's a permanent gift. He says when He forgives, He separates your sins from you as far as the east is from the west."

They heard a noise behind them and turned to see Kendall with tears in her eyes. She came up and wrapped her arms around the two of them.

"Welcome to the family, Rachel!"

Then Kendall turned and called out to the others to tell them the news of Rachel's salvation. They all came to hug her and welcome her. Jesse stepped back to let them in. He bumped into Spence.

"It's a great feeling, ain't it?" the old cowboy asked. "Leading a lost lamb to the Shepherd. There's nothing quite like it."

The old man peered at Jesse.

"You know, you look like you're carrying quite a load yourself, young man. You let me know if you ever want to talk about it, you hear?"

"Rachel, you told me you want to learn control. Tell me what you think is your biggest problem with control."

Esther and Rachel sat on a bench at the side of the dojo, resting from their workout. Rachel could see that her knowledge of self-defense moves had impressed her new teacher. Now she needed to find a way to express her fear of losing control without telling Esther what happened with Colin. She sat in silent thought for a moment, struggling to put it into words.

"I've known martial arts since I was a child," Rachel began. "My father and uncle felt this world can be a dangerous place and wanted me to know how to protect myself.

But when I get scared, I panic and just start reacting."

Esther nodded.

"Fear can make us lose control. Yet, that's when we need control most of all."

She reached under the bench and pulled her purse onto the bench next to her. Esther's hand dug in the purse until she pulled out a small, blue New Testament. She riffled through the pages until she came to a verse.

"I was so excited to hear that you have accepted Christ as your Savior. You will find that the Bible holds the answers to your questions, and even your fears. Let me show you these verses in 2 Peter 1."

Rachel took the proffered Bible and read the verses silently. Something about the words triggered a memory.

Her uncle had her in a firm hold. Even though she knew her uncle would never hurt her, Rachel felt panic swell inside. She began to feel claustrophobic. Instead of "tapping out" to signify her surrender, Rachel began to struggle and lash out. One hand caught her uncle on the side of his head. She saw the surprise and hurt when he released her and rubbed his fingers over the spot.

"Rachel, you know the right moves, but you must *learn self-control! You panicked just then, didn't you?"*

She looked down so she wouldn't have to see the disappointment in her teacher's eyes. When he asked her again if she had panicked, she just nodded. Tears stung her eyes.

She felt his hand rest gently on her shoulder. When Rachel looked up, she didn't see disappointment, just loving concern.

"Come sit with me," he told her, motioning to a spot on the mat.

Teacher and student sat in silence for a moment, then Uncle Jon drew out his pocket New Testament. Rachel knew he kept the small book with him all the time and often referred to it during his day.

"Rachel, there is a verse in here that addresses self-control. Here, read this yourself and you'll see what I mean."

He handed her the Testament and pointed to a verse near the back of the book. She read silently for a moment, then looked at him with a question in her expression.

"Did you see it?"

She shook her head.

"Right here," he pointed to the verses. "It says "add to your faith virtue, to virtue knowledge, to knowledge self-control.'"

Uncle Jon caught Rachel's gaze with his own.

"You have knowledge. Now you must add self-control. This is vital, Rachel. If you don't have self-control you could injure yourself or someone else during a fight. It could also give your opponent the opportunity to use your panic against you."

He stood up and she stood with him. Uncle Jon drew her into a hug. When he released her he lifted her chin with gentle fingers.

"Continue growing in knowledge, Rachel, but add self-control to that knowledge."

"Rachel?"

Rachel came back to the present. Esther was staring at her with a concerned expression. Embarrassed that she had missed what her teacher was telling her, Rachel shook her head.

"I'm sorry, Esther. The words you showed me reminded me of a time when my Uncle Jon was trying to teach me the same thing. I guess I was reliving that time."

Esther chuckled.

"I do that all the time. Sounds like this is something

you've dealt with for a long time."

Rachel blew out a frustrated breath.

"Yes, and I don't know what to do about it. I'm fine until I get in a situation that scares me. Then all sense of self-control flies out the window."

Esther took Rachel's hand and squeezed it.

"We'll work on that together, okay?"

Rachel nodded.

"Thanks, Esther. I need all the help I can get."

Chapter Eight

Rachel dug through her top drawer, searching for the small sewing kit she had brought with her. With an exasperated sigh she closed the drawer and stood with her elbows on top of the dresser. Where had she left that kit? The hem had started to come out on her favorite top and she wanted to fix it before Jesse arrived. They were planning a trip to town to have lunch with David and Christy. She normally worked half-days on Saturdays, but Kendall had told her to take the whole day off.

Rachel was looking forward to visiting with the sweet couple that had taken her in when she arrived in Forrestville.

She glanced at her dog laying contentedly in a sunbeam coming through the window. Angel looked completely relaxed, yet Rachel knew that if the Border Collie heard something outside, she would come to her feet in a flash.

"Angel, do you know where that sewing kit is?"

Rachel shook her head.

"Never mind, why would you know?"

An idea began to form. She might not have taken it out of the suitcase when she unpacked. Rachel turned and headed for the open closet. She grabbed the suitcase handle and pulled the bag out of the closet, laying it on the bed so she could get to it easily. When she opened the bag, she didn't see the sewing kit, so she began to run her hands through the pockets on the sides.

She found the kit when a pin protruding from it stuck her finger.

"Ow!"

Rachel stuck the finger in her mouth, then examined it for bleeding. Something else in the suitcase caught her eye. A small velvet pouch was in one of the inside pockets, sitting in a corner.

That pouch did not look familiar. She picked it up, the sewing kit forgotten. Stepping over to her dresser, Rachel opened the pouch and gently poured the contents out on a scarf that was laying on her dresser. She saw a gleam of gold and red with a twinkle of diamonds. She caught her breath at the extravagance of the ladybug pendant. How had this gotten in her suitcase?

She stood for a moment, thinking about the day she packed the suitcase. Rachel knew she did not own anything like this pendant.

Had Colin put this in her suitcase? Why? If he had wanted to give it to her, he would have just offered it to her. Rachel wondered if Colin hid it when he broke into her cottage. She examined the pendant again, thinking this must be a very expensive piece of jewelry.

There was a knock at her door, then Jesse's voice.

"Rachel? Are you ready to go? I'm not sure I'm brave enough to ride in your rust bucket. Let's take my truck. It's a lot safer."

Jesse closed the cabin door and stopped to scratch Angel behind the ears. Then he stuck his head in her bedroom.

"Hey, you ready?"

He stopped when he saw her standing by her dresser, her attention riveted on a piece of jewelry on top of the dresser. Rachel looked up at him with a touch of fear in her eyes.

"What's wrong?"

"This isn't my necklace."

Rachel waved Jesse over to look at the item.

"I think it was stolen, but I don't know how it got in my suitcase. What can I do?"

Jesse picked up the pendant and studied it for a moment, admiring the glint of gold and enamel, then handed it back to Rachel.

"Let's take it to Maggie Jones. She's our police chief. Maggie can check into it for you. She helped me a lot when I was in trouble and helped me get on at the Rocking K."

Rachel shrank from involving the police, but realized that was the only thing she could do. She didn't want to be responsible for this valuable piece of jewelry. She thought about what had happened in her cottage and decided she didn't want to hide anymore.

Jesse stood quietly beside her, waiting for her decision. Finally, Rachel nodded.

"Yeah, I think I need to talk to her."

She looked into Jesse's intense brown eyes. It was so easy to get lost in those eyes. Rachel looked down at her hands as she smoothed the velvet pouch.

"I think I need to tell her the whole story."

"Hey, Jesse! It's good to see you. Who is this with you?"

Maggie Jones' voice was warm and gracious. Rachel thought this must be the friendliest town she had ever been in.

"This is my friend and our new cook, Rachel James. And this lady is my friend, Police Chief Maggie Jones."

Rachel reached out to shake Maggie's hand; a little in awe of the woman in front of her. She was very impressed that Maggie was already a Police Chief. Rachel always thought of police chiefs as being old men, ready to retire. Maggie looked to be in her early forties.

"Welcome to Forrestville, Rachel. I bet Kendall is glad to have you. Cooking and housework are not her strong suits."

Maggie laughed and Jesse joined her. Rachel managed a small chuckle.

The police chief waved them to the chairs in front of her desk as she moved to sit behind it.

"What can I do for you today?"

Rachel looked at Jesse, who nodded to her. She took the small velvet pouch out of her purse and handed it to Maggie.

"I found this in my suitcase a little while ago. It was hiding in a pocket. It's not mine and I don't know how it got there."

She took a deep breath.

"I have an idea though."

Maggie took the necklace out, admired it briefly, then eased it back into the pouch. She waited quietly for Rachel to continue, her blue eyes kind and encouraging.

Rachel took another breath, then began.

"A few months ago I killed a man."

When the police chief sat forward, her gaze zeroed in on her, Rachel had to swallow hard to be able to go on. Then she told Maggie the whole story - the attempted rape, her defense of herself, the flight, and how she wound up in Forrestville.

Just then a young boy stuck his head in the door.

"Hi Mom! I need to ask you about something.'

"Robert, didn't I tell you to knock before you open that door?"

Maggie's voice was stern, but the boy just grinned impishly.

"Sorry, I forgot. I'll just wait out here." His head disappeared and the door closed. Maggie shook her head; an exasperated look on her face.

"I'm sorry for the interruption. That's my son, Robert. He's been bugging me to buy him a flash drive to store his music and videos on. Please, go on."

Rachel sighed and sagged in her chair a little.

"That's it."

Maggie got up and came around her desk. She laid her hand on Rachel's shoulder.

"You did the right thing, coming to me. After hearing your story, I suspect you would not be charged with anything, Rachel. It sounds like a pretty clear case of self-defense."

Rachel pointed at the pouch on Maggie's desk.

"What about that?"

"Let me hold on to it for now. I'll look into it and find who it belongs to."

"Will they think I took it? Will I be in trouble?"

Rachel's voice trembled just a bit.

"Not at all. They don't even have to know you're involved."

Maggie looked into Rachel's eyes.

"You're not planning to run again, are you?"

Rachel just shook her head.

"Let me check into things, then get back with you. If you'll give me your cell phone number I'll call you."

Maggie's words encouraged Rachel. She felt like a huge load had been lifted off of her.

"Thanks, Chief Jones."

"You're quite welcome. Just call me Maggie. Everyone else does. Come on, I'll walk you out."

As they walked out of the office, Robert's face peeked around the corner.

"Mom, can I talk to you now?"

"Go on in my office, son. I'll be there in a minute."

Robert sat in his mother's chair while he waited for her to walk the couple out. He saw the velvet pouch laying on her desk and wondered what was in it. The boy knew he was not supposed to touch anything on his mother's work desk, but curiosity won. He got up and peeked out the door. Maggie was still standing in the lobby talking to the man and woman that had been in her office.

He quickly sat at her desk again and picked up the pouch. It felt heavy in his hand. He opened it and dumped out the contents. Robert's eyes widened at the sight of the enameled pendant. He picked it up off the desk and turned it round and round in his hands. He saw a place on the back that had a piece that slid open. Curious now, he played with the piece, sliding it back and forth. When the piece seemed to stick, he abandoned playing with it and pretended to make the ladybug fly.

The boy was so preoccupied with his game, he didn't notice the tiny flash drive that fell out and landed on the blotter. After a few passes of the "flying" ladybug, Robert lost interest and carefully placed it back inside the pouch. He laid the pouch where he found it, then sat back to wait for his mother.

The bored child was just at the point of grabbing a pencil and doodling on the calendar blotter when he saw a very small bright red flash drive. The way it sat on the desk made him think his mom had laid it there just for him.

"All right!" Robert pumped a fist in the air. "She got me my own flash drive."

He snatched it up and shoved it in his pocket. Then he dashed out the door and down the hall to the lobby. When he got to his mother, he threw his arms around her in a brief, fierce hug.

"Thanks, Mom!" he blurted. "Gotta go now. See you at home."

Before Maggie could get a word out, Robert was out the door and running down the street. She saw him meet up with another boy, then turn to go to the park. She knew it would be a couple of hours before he arrived at the house.

"Thanks for what?"

Chapter Nine

Jacquelyn ended her call and set the cell phone on her desk in her bedroom. The anger that began when she found that Colin had stolen from her was growing inside like a fire. When he returned the necklace - and he *would* return the necklace; she would make sure of that - she planned to kill him anyway. No one stole from her and got away with it.

She reached for the call button on her intercom.

"Brock, is Colin Taylor here?"

When she received an affirmative answer, she narrowed her eyes and thought for a moment.

"Leave him in the living room and come up here for a moment. I have something I want you to do."

When her assistant entered the room, he hesitated. Jacquelyn knew he felt strange about conducting business in her bedroom. However, she had made plain to him from day one that business was *all* that would be done in that room. Jacquelyn was not interested in starting a relationship. All of her energies went toward building her own little empire.

"Brock, I am not completely confident Mr. Taylor will get my property back to me. I don't think he is as serious as I am about getting that necklace back."

"When I meet with him to get his report on his progress, I want you to put a tracker on him and on his car. Then add a little something special to the car. I want him to know I mean business."

The big man grinned.

"I'll be happy to follow Mr. Taylor. I'd be happy to finish him off for you, if you want."

Jacquelyn slowly shook her head as a sinister smile spread across her face.

"No, don't kill him. I want you to follow him, though. Make sure he finds the young woman he *says* has my pendant. After we retrieve the necklace, I want to kill Mr. Taylor myself."

Brock went to a drawer and withdrew two small tracking devices and a small square box.

"I'll put one in his cell phone and the other on his car. How about I put the 'special something' near the gas tank?"

"That will do nicely, yes. Tell him he has to leave his phone with you while he is in conference with me. He can get it back when he leaves. While you're following him, make sure to report back to me each day."

Jacquelyn smiled in anticipation. She couldn't wait to get her hands on the necklace and its contents. The sale of the flash drive would provide her with a very large sum of money. Jacquelyn liked having lots of money.

"Mr. Taylor, have you made any progress in finding the young woman who has my property?"

Colin blinked and fidgeted as he avoided looking at Jacquelyn. Finally, he dared to look up and tried pasting on a charming smile.

"I think so," he hedged. "I'm checking with a couple of

associates who may have seen or heard about her. I should know something in a few days. Then I'll go find her and get the necklace back."

Jacquelyn held his gaze while she tapped her lacquered nails on the top of her desk. Finally, she stood and walked around the desk. She sat in the chair next to Colin and laid a hand on his knee. The scent of her expensive perfume might have been enticing if he hadn't been so nervous. Colin barely managed to keep from shrinking from her.

"Mr. Taylor," she almost purred. "I want to make sure you understand how serious this situation is. That pendant means a lot to me. I am deeply grieved that you chose to steal from me."

Jacquelyn began to squeeze just above his knee. As Colin began to squirm in pain, she reached with her other hand to grab his chin. Pulling his face around so that she could look him directly in the eye, she exerted an extra bit of pressure on the knee.

"I want you to know I take this very seriously, Colin. I want you to take it seriously too."

With that she released his chin and his knee; then she curved her fingers and ran her nails down his wrist and hand, leaving bleeding scratches marking his skin. Colin gaped at the wounds as she returned to her desk chair and stared at him coldly.

"I think you will find that I do not play around. When you find the young woman and retrieve the necklace, you will call me. I will arrange a meeting place for you to return my property to me. Do you understand?"

Rubbing his sore knee, Colin nodded sullenly.

"I said, do you understand me? Answer out loud, please."

"Yes, I understand."

"Very good. You are dismissed."

Colin left Jacquelyn's house wishing he had never met the woman.

Colin fumed all the way home. How dare that woman manhandle him! How dare she dismiss him as if he were her minion! He couldn't wait until he could give her that blasted necklace and be done with her.

Underneath the anger, however, was a strong thread of fear. Whenever he thought about her icy blue eyes holding his gaze, Colin experienced chills all over. He had no doubt this woman was quite serious about retrieving that necklace.

As he rubbed his sore knee, Colin found himself wondering why she was so adamant about getting that pendant back. Sure, it was pretty and expensive, but it didn't seem all that priceless. And he didn't see her being sentimental about it, or anything else for that matter.

He shook his head. Never mind why, he told himself. Just find Rachel, get the necklace, give it back, and get as far as possible from Jacquelyn Marquette.

Colin pulled into his uncle's circular drive with a sigh of relief. All he wanted to do right now was take a long hot shower and relax. Maybe he could persuade his uncle to watch a movie with him. They both liked old Westerns. He'd have to see what was on.

Jacquelyn kept an eye on the monitor that showed Colin's location. Her sense of anticipation grew as he drew-closer to his home. The screen was split so that she could see where Colin, or rather his phone, was and where the car was.

She saw that the car had stopped. After waiting a few minutes, she could see the car was still in the same location, but Colin had moved away from it.

Her fingers flew over her cell phone.

Colin got out of his car and waved to his uncle as he approached the front door.

"How was your day today, Uncle Marcus?" he called out. "You feel like watching a good Western?"

His uncle's reply was lost in a loud *BOOM* behind Colin. A hot blast pushed him forward and onto his knees. His uncle was knocked backward through the door and into the house. Several windows shattered, the shards flying into the front rooms of the house.

Colin staggered to his feet, his knees almost buckling with pain. He stared in horrified disbelief at his prized automobile, which was now a raging fireball. Vaguely he could hear the wail of his uncle's security alarms screaming behind him..

"Are you okay?"

His ears were ringing as he looked into Marcus' eyes which were wide with shock. His uncle's arm came around his shoulders, helping him into the house.

"Come inside and sit down. Let me take a look at those knees. You took a pretty hard fall, there."

Colin let himself be led into the house and placed in a chair. Outside he could hear the muffled tones of household staff as someone called the fire department while others rushed to put out the fire. Marcus settled him in a chair and when to get a first aid kit.

While his uncle was gone, Colin felt a vibration at his waist. In his shocked state he wasn't sure what was happening, then he realized his phone had received a text notification. He reached for the device and entered his password. When he read the text, Colin felt the blood drain from his face.

"I told you I meant business. Next time it might not be just your car."

Attached was a picture of Uncle Marcus in front of their home.

"Colin, what's going on?"

Colin looked up into his uncle's angry face. He knew Marcus had a right to be angry. He also had a right to know the whole story, but Colin didn't plan to tell him. He was afraid his uncle would throw him out and disinherit him if he knew the extent of his nephew's extra activities and why someone blew up his car.

He returned his cell phone to its holster with shaking fingers and kept his head down in an attempt to avoid answering.

"I asked you a question, son. I need an answer."

Marcus sat across from Colin, his gaze boring into his nephew. The expression on his face told the young man that he would need to give a good explanation for the events of the past hour.

Colin sighed and put his head in his hands. Then he sat up and looked his uncle in the eye.

"Uncle Marcus, I'm in a lot of trouble."

Before his uncle could say anything, Colin hurried to explain.

"I can't tell you anything more about it right now. The important thing right now is for me to go find Rachel and get, I mean, and make sure she's okay."

Marcus gave him a suspicious look.

"What does your finding Rachel have to do with your car exploding? What kind of trouble have you gotten into?"

Colin mentally berated himself. He should have known his uncle would connect the two if he said anything about finding Rachel at this point. How was he going to get out of this one?

"I, I made someone mad," he improvised. "I need to get out of town for a while to let her, uh, him settle down. I think I have a lead on where Rachel might be, so I could use this time to go find her and check on her."

Marcus shook his head.

"I don't know what I'm going to do with you, Colin. I'm going to want more of an explanation of the trouble you're in at some point in the future. Right now I want to know how you got this lead on Rachel."

"A friend of a friend told me about a cousin of his in Louisiana who might have seen her. I'd like to go check it out."

Marcus looked out his shattered front window at the smoking hulk of Colin's car. His gaze returned to his nephew, who sat sweating and hoping that he wouldn't ask any more questions.

"All right. You can use the extra car in the garage. Make sure to check the battery, gas, and tires; it's been sitting unused for a while. Let me know if you find Rachel and if she needs anything."

Here, the older man fixed a stern glare on his nephew.

"Remember what I told you earlier. If I find out you had anything to do with her leaving, you and I are going to have a serious talk. Do you understand my meaning?"

Colin swallowed hard.

"Yes, sir."

Chapter Ten

Jesse and Rachel walked silently toward the diner after leaving Maggie's office.

"You okay?"

Jesse glanced at Rachel's profile. She looked as if she was deep in thought. She nodded once without looking at him.

Just as Jesse was about to speak again, he saw a small, elderly woman approaching them with a determined frown on her wrinkled face. He felt his stomach drop, knowing what was coming. Mrs. Bronson never had anything good to say about anyone in town, but she seemed to have a special hatred for Jesse and never missed an opportunity to ream him out about his past.

"Young woman, do you know who your companion is?"

Mrs. Bronson's question was aimed at Rachel, but her glare was fixed on Jesse. Rachel looked up from her reverie with a start.

"Ma'am?"

"I said, do you know who this man is? Or, I should say, *what* he is? He's a drug dealing thug! I don't know what our Police Chief is thinking letting him roam the streets free as a bird. It is very unwise for you to keep company with a man like that. You will harm your reputation if you are seen with him."

Jesse felt his face and neck redden. It seemed that no matter how hard he worked, how eager he was to make things right, it would never be enough - especially for Mrs. Bronson.

"Ma'am, I don't see what right you have to say those things about Jesse. I have found him to be a gentleman at all times. I've seen him working hard at the ranch, always willing to help someone."

Rachel's words had no more effect on the old gossip than pebbles on granite. The elderly woman shook her finger in Rachel's face.

"You just watch yourself, young lady. This man is not to be trusted!"

With that Mrs. Bronson marched down the sidewalk, stopping in front of the bookstore. Before she went in the door, she turned and sent another venomous glare at Jesse and Rachel.

Jesse found his hands clenched at his side and forced himself to relax them. He sighed and hung his head.

"I'm sorry you had to hear all that."

Rachel laid her hand on his arm.

"Do you want to tell me about it? Why does that woman hate you so much?"

Jesse wanted to refuse. He was trying to leave that life behind him, despite people like Mrs. Bronson. But he realized that Rachel would eventually hear it from someone.

"A few years ago I was working for the town of Forrestville. I also worked for a local businessman, selling drugs. To the people of the town, he seemed like a nice, respectable businessman and council member. But he was actually a drug lord. I realized pretty quickly that the extra money I made did not make up for how bad I felt selling drugs to kids. But whenever I tried to leave, he would threaten

Aunt Abigail. Finally, he got caught trying to kill Esther. He was arrested for her brother's murder and for attempting to murder Esther and Ninja."

"How long did you sell drugs for him?"

Jesse looked up when he heard the strain in her voice.

"Just a little over a year. When my boss was arrested, I was freed from that life. Because I provided testimony against Grayson, I was given probation and sent to the Rocking K to work. I'm trying to put that life behind me now."

Jesse waited to see Rachel's reaction. She didn't look at him, just continued on her way to the diner. He began to feel angry. Finally he blurted out.

"You know, if you don't want anything to do with me now, I get it. Who wants to be seen with a former drug dealer, right?"

Rachel whipped around, her eyes shooting angry sparks. Jesse waited for her to tell him to get lost.

"I don't judge people without knowing the whole story, Jesse! Don't get all defensive with me. I just need to think about things, okay? I didn't say anything about not wanting to be seen with you. So, just, shut up and let me think!"

"Fine, I'll leave you alone."

Jesse stalked down the street, just ahead of Rachel. As they walked, he began to cool down a little. It wasn't Rachel's fault that old biddy had to drag his business out right there on the sidewalk.

Just before they got to the diner, Jesse stopped and turned to face Rachel.

"I'm sorry I got defensive with you. I know I shouldn't. I just can't help it when someone brings up my past. But I shouldn't have gotten mad at you."

Rachel looked up into his hurt eyes.

"I'm not judging you, Jesse. As far as I can see, you've made a complete turnaround. Besides, who am I to judge you? I killed a man, remember?"

Jesse gazed into her sweet face, getting lost in the care and concern in her warm brown eyes. He realized he was more than a little attracted to her. Somehow it seemed right, although he didn't see how Rachel could possibly feel the same way about him.

Jesse reached to open the diner door. He still felt tension between Rachel and him, but didn't know what else he could do.

Jesse and Rachel entered the diner and immediately spotted David and Christy sitting at what had to be their favorite spot. The older couple looked up with welcoming smiles and waved them over.

Rachel hugged Christy while David and Jesse shook hands. They sat around the table and scanned the menus.

"I am so hungry I feel like I could eat just about anything on this menu," Rachel joked. She gave a little shudder.

"Except the Brussels sprouts. I can't stand those!"

Jesse agreed with her.

"I wonder whoever thought those things were fit to eat?"

Christy swatted his arm.

"I'll have you know there are some people in this world who actually enjoy eating Brussels sprouts."

Then she gave a mischievous grin.

"However, I am not one of them."

They all laughed and then greeted the young waitress who came to take their order.

"I'll bring your drinks in just a few minutes," she promised as she gathered the menus.

After the waitress left, Rachel got up from her chair.

"Please excuse me. I need to visit the ladies' room."

Christy stood up too.

"I think I'll go too, before the food arrives."

David shook his head as he watched his wife follow Rachel to the restrooms.

"What is it with women and visiting the restroom together?" he laughed.

Then he turned his attention to Jesse. His hazel eyes bored into the young man with a concerned look.

"You okay? You seem pretty tense."

Jesse started to say he was fine, then found himself blurting out the whole story about Mrs. Bronson accosting them."

"Good grief, that woman is something else!" David exclaimed.

Jesse could think of several "somethings" to describe the woman, but he realized his thoughts were not right.

David stared at him.

"She really got to you, didn't she?"

Jesse nodded miserably.

"David, it seems like no matter what I do, how much good I try to do, it's never enough. I'll always be a drug dealer in their eyes."

"Good enough for who?"

Jesse was startled.

"What do you mean?"

"I mean who are you trying to be good enough for?"

David reached across the table to lay his hand on Jesse's shoulder.

"Jesse, the people who are important, the people who care, already know the fine man you have become and the godly man you are growing into. They know you have a kind and loving heart. I heard how you led Rachel to Christ and have helped her to grow in the faith. She is positively glowing."

The younger man started to protest but David raised his hand to stop him.

"There will always be people who will have negative things to say about you. They just seem to have the need to tear others down. Don't take it personally. They talk that way about everybody.

David leaned back in his seat, his attention still on Jesse.

"You know that when you accepted Christ you were forgiven for all of your sins, including the drug dealing. Are you now trying to earn that forgiveness? Because if you are, you need to stop. God extended His full forgiveness to you; you can't do a thing to earn it, you just accept it by faith. That's why it's called grace."

Jesse started to reply but cut it off when they saw the women returning.

David caught his eye.

"Just think about what I said, okay?"

"It is so good to see you again!"

Abigail squeezed her nephew as tightly as she could, then stepped back to look him over, her dark eyes filled with loving concern.

"Are you doing all right? Are you getting enough to eat? You look like you've lost some weight and you have dark circles under your eyes."

Jesse squirmed at his aunt's probing questions and tried to divert her.

"Aunt Abigail, I'd like you to meet Rachel James. Rachel, this is my aunt, Abigail Matthews."

"Rachel, I am so glad to finally meet you. Jesse brags about your cooking all the time."

The older woman shot a fond glance at her nephew.

"He says it's almost as good as mine."

Rachel laughed.

"I wouldn't go quite that far, Ms. Matthews. He brags about your cooking too. He's even shared a few of your chocolate chip cookies."

"Just call me Aunt Abigail, child. And I will be happy to bake you some of those cookies any time you like."

Abigail turned her attention to Jesse.

"Now, don't think introducing me to your lovely friend here will distract me from those questions I asked you. Are you getting enough to eat? Are you getting enough sleep at night?"

Jesse had to smile at her motherly tone as they settled on the couch, with Rachel taking the nearby armchair.

"I'm fine, Aunt Abs. I have lost some weight, even though our new cook serves us great food at all our meals, including some great desserts."

He grinned at Rachel.

"We're just working extra hard and sweating it off, I guess. You know I usually lose weight in the summer."

His hope he could head off any further questions about his health turned out to be in vain. Aunt Abigail just peered more closely at his face.

"What about those dark circles? I know what that means. You're *not* getting enough sleep. Are you still trying to do your work and everybody else's? Still trying to earn forgiveness?"

Jesse was startled at his aunt's words and embarrassed that she would bring that up in front of his guest. He tried to catch his aunt's eye and give a subtle head shake to end the questioning. Abigail ignored his silent signals and pursued her line of questioning.

"Son, everyone can see that you're trying to earn forgiveness."

"What do you mean I'm trying to *earn* forgiveness?"

Abigail sighed as she looked up, as if for wisdom in dealing with this foolish youth. She looked him straight in the eye.

"Jesse, ever since you decided to leave the drug trade and start living for the Lord, you've been trying to earn the grace and forgiveness God gave you. You've been taking on every job and doing everything people ask of you, trying to prove to the whole town that you're not the same man you were back then."

Her nephew sat in thoughtful silence for a moment. Wise woman that she was, Abigail gave him time to think about what she said, instead of continuing to talk or ask him questions. Rachel watched the conversation in a respectful silence that endeared her to Abigail. Finally, the older woman slid an arm around Jesse's shoulders and pulled him into a tight hug. She leaned back to look in his face.

"Young man, you can't wear yourself out trying to earn the forgiveness and respect of everyone in this town. You just have to let go of the past and move forward. God has forgiven you already. That's all you need to know. That's all *anyone* needs to know."

Jesse kissed her on the cheek, then got up and moved to look out the front window. Although it was a sunny, beautiful day outside, he didn't see anything. All he could see was the old woman who berated him and Rachel. All he could hear was her hate-filled words reminding him about his past as a drug dealer.

Abigail watched him with loving concern. She knew her boy was hurting; she just didn't know why.

"Do you want to talk about it, sweetheart?"

Jesse turned toward her with a sad smile. He glanced at Rachel, then at the clock on the wall.

"Maybe another time, Aunt Abs. Right now, we need to get on back to the ranch. It's almost time for evening chores. I just wanted to come by to see you and introduce you to Rachel."

He grinned impishly.

"I also hoped to snag a few of your chocolate chip cookies. Rachel's a great cook, but nobody makes chocolate chip cookies like yours."

Abigail laughed and led her nephew to the kitchen where she bagged up a dozen of her cookies.

"I just baked these this morning," she declared. "I must have known deep down that you were coming."

She looked at Rachel with an impish grin of her own, then bagged another dozen of the sweet treats. Abigail reached into one of the drawers and pulled out a large index card with writing.

"After hearing about you from him, I was hoping my nephew would bring you to visit. I even fixed up a card with the recipe for these cookies."

Abigail handed the cookies to Rachel, then pulled her into a welcoming hug. Rachel thanked her and returned the hug.

"I think I'll go get the truck cooling off. Jesse, come on out when you're ready."

After Rachel left, Abigail gave her nephew another hug, her face beaming with joy.

"You bring Rachel with you any time you like. I can tell she's a very special young lady."

Jesse blushed. He didn't know why, but hearing his aunt speak well of his friend made him feel warm all over. He felt like something momentous had happened here today with these two important women in his life.

"Is there something I should know?"

Jesse came to himself with a start. When had Rachel become so special to him? He couldn't let her in like that. Rachel was a sweet, innocent girl. She deserved better than an ex-drug dealer.

"We're just friends, Aunt Abs. She's a sweet girl, but we're just friends."

And maybe, just maybe, if he kept telling himself that, he would start to believe it.

Chapter Eleven

Robert inserted his new flash drive into the USB port on his home computer. He was excited to have his own storage device. His mom didn't believe in giving kids lots of electronic gadgets. He had a laptop computer to help with his homework, a basic cell phone so he could call his mom if needed, and now a flash drive he could use to store and carry his music.

Now he could listen to his music during study hall. Mrs. Norton allowed students to listen to music on the school's computers while they studied or did homework as long as they used headphones or ear buds. They also had to keep the music turned down. If she could hear it, the guilty party got one warning. If she heard it again, she would make the student turn it off. If she heard if after that, the device was confiscated.

Robert wished his mom would get him an MP3 player. Then he could listen wherever he wanted, instead of having to be at a computer. Maybe he would ask for one for Christmas. He didn't really have a long wish list this year. Just an MP3 player and a dog. He figured his chances of getting even one of those were pretty slim. His chances of getting both - well, Christmas was still several months away. He would work on his mom during that time.

His hand manipulated the mouse to pull up the drive. He would see what the computer called it, then rename it. As lines of numbers filled the screen, Robert squinted in disbelief. What's this junk on here? This was supposed to be a new flash drive.

"Hey, son, I'm home. Let me get changed, then I'll get started on dinner."

Robert flashed a grin at his mother.

"Okay. Thanks again for the flash drive. But I don't think it's new. It has some kind of junk on it."

Maggie stood behind Robert and focused on the screen.

"Robert, I didn't get you a flash drive. Remember, I said I would think about it. Where did you get this one?"

The youngster squirmed in his chair, suddenly very intent on the screen. His hand started to reach for the delete button.

"Stop!"

Maggie's voice was sharp. She moved his hand away from the computer, then took a firm hold of his shoulder and turned him to face her.

"I asked you a question, young man. Where did you get the flash drive and why did you think it came from me?"

Robert lifted his gaze to meet the stern expression on his mother's face. He talked fast, hoping she would understand why he took something from her desk.

"While you were talking to Jesse and that lady, I sat at your desk. I sort of opened that velvet pouch and sort of played with the necklace inside. Did you know it had a place on the back that opened? When I put the necklace back, I saw the flash drive on your calendar. Since it was on your desk and that's what I was coming to talk to you about, well, I sort of thought it was mine."

Maggie sighed and pinched the bridge of her nose.

"Son, you know I've told you to leave things alone on my desk at work. You could contaminate evidence that way. Hop up and let me see what's on that flash drive. You go clean up and set the table for us."

While Robert followed her instructions, Maggie scrolled through the contents of the flash drive. As she read through the material, she realized that it contained information from a large pharmaceutical company. She dismounted the drive and held it in her hand to examine it.

Maggie could see how the small red drive could easily hide inside the ladybug pendant. She closed her hand around it and thought for a minute, with her head bowed and her eyes closed.

Her head came up as she remembered her friend, Monica, who had just gotten a promotion at the Shreveport FBI office. Maggie strode into the living room and searched through her purse until she found the new business card Monica had sent her.

Maggie and Monica had gone to Police Academy together. When they finished, Maggie became an officer in the Shreveport Police Department. Monica worked for the Bossier City Police Department for several years before joining the FBI. They stayed in touch, getting together as often as possible to celebrate each other's triumphs and encourage each other through the hard times.

"Mom, what's for dinner? I'm starved!"

Robert stuck his head in the door of his room. He wore the sheepish expression of a child who expected to be punished, but hoped he could postpone it as long as possible. Maggie waved him over. She put her hands on his shoulders so she could look him in the eye.

"Robert, you know you did wrong to meddle with stuff on my desk, don't you?"

The boy nodded; his eyes wide.

Maggie thought for a minute, then gave him a smile.

"I won't punish you this time, but I want you to remember to not tamper with or touch anything on my desk at the Police office. Now, I'm hungry too. I think we have a pizza in the freezer that we really need to bake and eat. What do you say?"

Robert cheered while Maggie gave him a quick hug. Normally she would have grounded him, but it was possible the boy had found an important piece of evidence that Maggie would have missed. She would call Monica after dinner and tell her all about the mysterious ladybug pendant, the young woman who found it, and the very interesting information contained in the flash drive.

Chapter Twelve

"No, no, NO!"

Colin shouted curses as he felt his car begin to bump and wobble. He pulled to the side of the narrow road and parked. The car shook with the force of Colin's door slam.

Kneeling beside the flat tire, Colin let loose with another long string of profanity. He jerked himself upright and went to get the spare and the jack. When he opened the trunk and stared into the well where the spare rested, he swore again. The spare was also flat. He had a sudden memory of his uncle telling him to get the spare replaced before he took his trip and him dismissing Uncle Marcus with a wave of his hand.

Discovering where Rachel was hiding had turned out to not be as hard as he had feared. Colin thought about the conversation with his source.

"Hey Colin, you should hear about this fighting chick. My cousin that lives in Shreveport told me his best friend works at a ranch in a dinky little town in Louisiana. One of the cowboys tried to make some moves on this good-looking girl. Ha! She beat the snot out of him and 'bout choked him out."

Colin rubbed his neck at the memory of Rachel choking him. He got the name of the town from the garrulous young man who wanted to talk more about the fight. Colin wasn't interested in hearing any more about the fight. He wanted to know the name of the dinky little town.

After seeing the text from Jacquelyn and persuading his uncle to let him go in search for Rachel, Colin felt he couldn't get out of town fast enough. He didn't bother to check out the car, he just loaded up his luggage and left.

Colin kicked the flat tire and looked up at the sky.

"Why do things like this always happen to me?" he groaned. "I have to get that blasted necklace back from Rachel. But I can't do that until I get to that dinky town and find her. I can't find her if this stupid car doesn't work!"

He stared down the long, empty roadway. In this rural area, it could be hours before anyone would come by. He glanced at his phone again, hoping to see a signal. Not a single bar showed. He considered throwing the phone in his anger, but decided that would be a pretty stupid move.

Once he got the necklace back in his possession, he was supposed to call Jacquelyn to let her know he had it. She had told him she would meet him at a location she would choose to retrieve her property.

The sun was high in the sky and Colin was already sweating profusely. He reached for the cup of soda he had bought at the diner in Longview, and tipped it up to get a sip. All of the soda was gone and he had drunk the last of the melted ice. He threw the cup away and started down the road, turning to lock his car. There had to be a house or trailer or *something* on this road where he could use their phone to get someone to come change his tire.

After about half an hour, Colin was dizzy and sick from walking in the heat. He never spent time outside if he could help it. He preferred climate-controlled buildings where he never had to worry about being too hot or too cold. Now he was hot and nauseated.

Through the sweat running into his eyes Colin spotted a figure by the fence that ran parallel to the road.

"Hey, can you help me?"

Colin stumbled to the fence post and leaned on it, coming precariously close to getting scratched by the barbed wire attached to the post.

He watched the cowhand eye him with suspicion. Colin knew he looked different from most of the people around here. He was wealthy and he liked to dress the part. His clothes and shoes were always top of the line and very expensive. Of course, right now his clothes probably looked as bedraggled as he did.

Colin saw when the cowhand decided to take pity on him. The young man pulled out a paper cup and filled it with water from an insulated cooler.

"Here," he told Colin. "Drink it slow so it won't make you sick."

Colin accepted the cup gratefully and sipped the water, letting it slide down his parched throat. When the cup was empty he held it out to the cowhand in a silent plea. Soon the cup was filled again and Colin drank it a little more quickly than he had the first one.

"Where are you from mister?"

The cowboy had gone back to his fence work, but Colin could see he was curious.

"I'm just passing through on my way from out west," he evaded. "Say, do you know where I could find a phone? My car has a flat tire and the spare is no good. I'd also like to get somewhere cool. I don't feel so good."

Colin's new acquaintance thought for a moment, then gave a slight nod.

"You can come back to the ranch house with me."

"Don't you have a cell phone on you that I could use?"

"Nope."

Colin couldn't believe this kid was out here working in the heat with no cell phone. Then he thought about his phone with no bars of service showing. Maybe the kid couldn't get a signal either.

The cowboy started picking up his tools and loading them into a pickup truck. He came back with an old blanket which he laid across the barbed wire.

"Climb over," he ordered Colin.

Colin eyed the blanket with distaste. It was old, dusty, and smelled like horse. But it would keep him from getting stuck while he got on the side of the fence where the truck waited to take him to relief. Colin climbed over, then watched the cowhand remove the blanket and throw it in the back of the truck. He was relieved he would not have to share the front seat with that nasty thing.

"My name's Colin."

He held out his hand to his rescuer.

"What's yours?"

"Mine's Jason. I work at the Rocking K ranch."

"Will your boss mind me showing up like this?"

"Nah, Kendall's cool. She'll let you call the garage and probably invite you to stay for lunch."

Colin breathed a sigh of relief. He would have a cool place to wait for someone to come fix his car. Once his car was ready and he felt better, he'd be on his way to find Rachel.

"Jason, what are you doing at the house at this time of day? Didn't I tell you to take your lunch?"

Kendall gave her employee a stern glare before she noticed the man behind him.

"Who is this?"

Jason shrugged and made a vague motion toward Colin with his hand.

"This is Colin. He got lost and got too hot. I thought you'd want me to bring him up here so he could cool off."

Colin stepped forward and held out his hand for Kendall to shake. He could see the suspicion in her eyes, but felt he could charm his way out of any situation. Then he remembered Jacquelyn's cold eyes and shuddered. Almost any situation, he thought.

"I really appreciate your help. My car has a flat and my spare is bad. I'm not used to being out in the heat, so your man there really saved my skin. Do you have a phone I can use to call a tow truck?"

Kendall gave him a long look, then gestured toward a phone in the living room.

"You can use the phone in there. There's also a number for Willie's in Forrestville. His garage is closest."

She hesitated a moment.

"You're welcome to stay for lunch."

She turned her attention back to Jason.

"You can stay for lunch, Jason, but then I want you out there working on that fence. I don't want any calves getting out and getting run over on that road."

"But, Kendall, it's hot out there," he whined. "Can't I do some work in the barn this afternoon? Then I can get back to work on the fence early tomorrow, when it's not so hot."

She thought about it, then smiled.

"I tell you what. You can do as you asked. But, if a calf or cow gets out and gets hurt or killed, you can reimburse me out of your check. I'll even let you do it on an installment plan."

Jason scowled. He liked to spend his paycheck as soon

as he got it and usually ran out of money long before the next paycheck. He knew he could not afford to pay for a valuable animal.

"I'll go back after lunch," he muttered.

"That's a good idea. Now go ring the bell so everyone can come in and wash up. Rachel's out this afternoon, but she left some sandwiches and fruit salad. I think there's even a pan of brownies."

Jason brightened at the mention of the brownies. He turned to Colin.

"You're in luck, mister. Our cook makes the best brownies I ever ate.

Colin hardly heard him. All he could do was stand and wonder. Was their cook, Rachel, the woman he was looking for? He mulled it over while he called Willie's and made arrangements for them to pick him up at the ranch and take him to his car. Willie promised to bring a tire after getting the make, model, and year from Colin.

When the call was done, Colin followed the voices of the cowhands to a large bathroom where they were all washing their hands. As Colin washed, he thought about how he could get more information about their cook. Finally, he decided on the direct approach.

"Jason says your cook makes the best brownies."

He directed his question to an older cowboy, who just stared at him for a minute before nodding.

"Yep, she does."

"She sounds like someone I used to know. Maybe it's the same person. What can you tell me about her?"

"Mister, I don't talk about other people and I hope they don't talk about me."

With that the older man strode away, seating himself at a large farmhouse table.

"Don't mind Spence. He's just ornery that way sometimes. Says he doesn't want to gossip."

Colin turned toward the friendlier voice belonging to a young man with deep auburn hair and mischievous brown eyes.

"I'm Mark. I heard you talking to my dad."

"Willie's your father?"

Colin was careful to not look too eager for information about Rachel. He would chat with the young man about other things first, then come back around to the subject he was most interested in.

"Yeah, people are always surprised that I don't work with my dad at the garage. But cars just aren't my thing, you know? I've always liked horses and cattle, so Dad asked Kendall to give me a try. She's a great boss."

"Looks like she hires good people."

Now Colin saw his chance.

"Tell me about your cook. Is she as good with other food as she is with brownies?"

The young cowboy's eyes lit up.

"Oh, yeah! Since she came, we've been eatin' good! She's pretty and nice too. Except, she doesn't like to be grabbed. She and Jason really got into it when he grabbed her for messin' with the horse he was supposed to help break and train."

Colin listened with great interest as Mark gleefully provided the juicy details of the fight between the new cook and the cowhand who thought he was the next great horse trainer.

"Does Jason hold a grudge against her?" he asked.

"Nah. He did at first, but then Rachel fixed his favorite dinner and had a nice talk with him. I don't know what they talked about, but I think everything's been cool.

Even though he has to work on the fence since the fight, I think Jason respects her for whipping his . . ."

"Mark! You're holding everyone up while you chew on this man's ear. It's time for lunch."

Mark blushed and hurried to sit at the table. Kendall pointed to another spot and invited Colin to have a seat. Then they all bowed their heads while she said a brief blessing.

While his hostess prayed, Colin exulted. He had found Rachel! Now all he had to do was get that pendant back.

After lunch, the cowhands returned to their various duties. Kendall gave directions to Jason regarding the fencing, then turned her attention to Colin.

"Did Willie tell you when he'd be out to get you?"

Colin wiped his mouth and laid his napkin on his plate. He smiled at his hostess.

"He said it would be about four o'clock since he had a couple other people to take care of. I want to thank you for your kind hospitality. I'll try to stay out of the way."

Kendall eyed him for a moment, then gave a short nod. "You can tour the stables and the grounds around the house, if you want. Please stay away from the pastures and the corrals where my hands are working. We have a dog here too. She's a working dog, not for petting or playing."

Colin tried to hide his glee. If he could find where Rachel lived, he could slip in quietly and retrieve the necklace. He hoped she hadn't found it and sold it.

Mark came up behind him. Colin knew he had a great source of information here. He walked with the young cowhand to the door and stood at the back door, taking in the panorama of the ranch.

"So, does Rachel live in the house?"

Colin posed the question casually, as if not really interested in the answer.

"No, she has her own cabin, just beyond those trees." Mark gestured toward a small wooden cabin with a bright blue door. Flowers bloomed in a box under the front window.

Mark continued. "Most of us hands stay in the bunkhouse, but a couple have cabins, like Spence. He's the one that didn't want to talk to you. He . . ."

"Mark, don't you have chores to do?"

Kendall's voice was kind, but firm. Colin got the idea she didn't like Mark giving him so much information.

After Mark and Kendall moved in different directions to get back to work, Colin sauntered around the yard a little, giving the appearance of admiring the flower gardens and taking in the view of the pastures. When he felt sure no one would notice him, he sidled over to Rachel's cabin.

Using his ever-present case of tools, Colin was inside the cabin in a moment, quietly closing and locking the door. He swung his gaze around. Just like her cottage on his uncle's property, the cabin was plain and simple. There was a vase of wildflowers on the small kitchen table and a bowl of fruit on the counter. Colin did not see a television, but there was a bookcase full of books.

Moving into the bedroom, he saw a twin bed neatly made, a rocking chair, and a pine dresser with her decorative box and a framed photograph. Colin picked up the picture for a closer look. Rachel sat on the grass with a black and white dog in front of her. Both of them looked happy to be with the other.

He set down the picture and looked under her bed for the suitcase. All he saw was a little dust. Colin stood with his eyes closed for a moment, thinking. The closet! That was where she had kept the suitcase at her cottage. He opened the door to the small closet and found the suitcase on the floor, unzipped and open.

Colin searched through the pockets, his movements becoming more frantic as he realized the pouch with the necklace was no longer hidden in there. Muttering curses under his breath, he stood and kicked the suitcase. Just as he headed back to the living room, he heard voices at the door.

Rachel unlocked her cabin door while juggling the bag of leftovers from the diner. She pushed through, eager to set her load on the table. Before she was all the way inside, she spotted a man in her living room. Rachel felt like her heart stopped. This felt way too familiar, especially when she saw who it was. Then it registered.

"You're alive!"

The words burst from her lips before she knew what she was saying. Rachel's thoughts and feelings were jumbled. She was outraged at the man standing in front of her for breaking into her home - again. She was elated and relieved that he was not dead, that she had not killed him. And Rachel was afraid. Was he here to exact revenge for what she did to him?

"Hey Rachel, you forgot . ." Jesse bumped into her from behind.

"What's wrong?"

Then he saw the man in her cabin.

"Who are you and what are you doing in Rachel's cabin?"

Jesse turned to Rachel and saw that she was deathly pale. He hurried to put his arm around her for support. She gratefully leaned on him.

“This is him, Jesse.”

Rachel tried to stop trembling. Tears ran down her cheeks.

“This is the man I thought I killed. He’s alive. I didn’t kill anyone.”

Jesse guided Rachel to the couch, then stood to confront the intruder, who still stood in the door of Rachel’s bedroom.

“Rachel, I need to talk to you alone, please.”

Colin’s voice was desperate.

“It’s very important. Please!”

Jesse stood in front of Rachel, then turned to her with a question in her eyes. She looked back at him, then shook her head.

“Mr. Taylor, I have no desire to have any kind of a conversation alone with you anywhere or at any time. While I am very glad that you are alive and seem to have suffered no harm from our last, uh, encounter, I do not feel safe around you.”

Colin sputtered.

“You don’t feel safe around me? I’m the one that got choked out by you! But I didn’t come here for that. I don’t even care about that. I have urgent business I need to discuss with you. I promise you I am stone cold sober and I will not try to hurt you.”

Jesse stepped forward and got right in Colin’s face.

“The lady said she doesn’t want to talk to you. Now, scram before I call the police.”

Colin’s face registered anger and desperation. He slid out past Jesse, but called out to Rachel.

“Please just think about it, Rachel. It is vitally important that I talk to you alone. We can meet wherever you feel safe. Please, it really is important!”

After Colin left, Jesse sat beside Rachel on the small couch and put his arm around her. She leaned against him and sobbed until she was worn out.

"Rachel, are you afraid of him? You know we'll all protect you. We won't let him anywhere near you."

She sat up and wiped her face. Jesse was surprised to see a smile on her face.

"Yes, I'm still a little afraid of him, even though I can defend myself. But, that's not why I'm crying. I'm crying because, well, because God is good."

Jesse was puzzled.

"I don't get it. You're crying because God is good? What do you mean?"

"God is good, Jesse. I didn't kill that man. I didn't kill anyone. I know God forgave all of my sins, but thinking I had killed someone still weighed on me. God let me know I didn't kill anyone."

Jesse put his arm around her again and squeezed her shoulders. He looked down into her beautiful, tearful face and grinned.

"You're right, Rachel. God is good."

Chapter Thirteen

"Jacquelyn Marquette."

The words were crisp and the tone businesslike, yet Colin could hear a menacing undertone. He tried to get words out but his mouth felt parched.

"Well?"

Colin knew that Jacquelyn was well aware of who was on the phone. She enjoyed knowing she scared him. He finally regained use of his voice.

"Ms. Marquette, I've found Rachel James. She works at a ranch called the Rocking K just outside a small town called Forrestville."

"That's very good, Mr. Taylor. Have you gotten possession of the necklace yet?"

"Well," Colin searched for a way to tell what he needed to report without admitting failure.

"I'll take that to mean you have not."

Colin sighed.

"No, not yet. I was searching her cabin at the ranch when she walked in on me. She wouldn't let me talk to her."

"I'm not interested in excuses, Mr. Taylor. Get my necklace back."

With that the call was cut off. Colin stared at his phone and resisted the temptation to throw it against the wall.

That woman was arrogant, infuriating, and terrifying. He gripped the phone in his sweaty hands as he slid into the desk chair. Colin slumped forward and cradled his head in his hands.

He had to get that necklace back! If he couldn't steal it from Rachel, maybe he could appeal to her. Tell her it belonged to his mother or something.

Colin sat up. That was it! He would tell Rachel he bought it for his mother and had tucked it in the suitcase because, hmmm. He'd have to think about that one for a while. But, for now, he'd set up a surveillance outside the bed and breakfast. Rachel had to come to town eventually. He'd wait for a chance to talk to her, then pour on every ounce of charm he had. Surely she would return the necklace. He hoped.

Colin settled into his chair and lifted his coffee to his lips. He felt a shiver run down his spine. He moved the coffee away from his mouth and looked around. Ever since he had arrived in Forrestville, he had had the feeling he was being watched. He never saw anyone, but the feeling lingered.

Movement across the street caught Colin's eye and he stood up for a better look. Yes! Rachel was walking into a bookstore and she was alone. He sauntered across the street as if he was taking a leisurely walk. He actually wanted to run across the street and accost Rachel, but he knew that would not end well and he would not get the information he needed.

Rachel paid for her books, a deep sense of contentment and gratification filling her. She was learning so much from her new Bible and the books recommended for her by Kendall and the pastor at their church. Rachel was filled with awe at the idea of God loving and forgiving her. Finding out she had not killed Colin was an extra gift.

As she stepped out of the bookstore, Rachel's senses sharpened. Before she even heard his voice, she sensed a presence near her.

"Rachel!"

She turned toward the source of the harsh whisper and saw Colin standing near an alley.

"Please. Just give me a minute. It's vitally important."

Rachel had never seen Colin so humble nor so desperate. When she looked into his eyes the fear in them startled her. What had Colin so afraid?

"I'll talk to you, but we're staying where people can see us."

She gave him a sharp look.

"Don't get any ideas, though. I will defend myself if necessary."

"Rachel, I don't want to hurt you. I just need that necklace."

She stepped back again and looked him over. Colin had dark circles around his eyes. Every few minutes he would run his trembling hand through his hair. The suave, well-dressed man she was used to seeing was now rumpled and disheveled, his hair sticking out in all directions and his clothes wrinkled and stained. Rachel wondered what had happened to him to change his appearance so drastically.

"I don't have it anymore. When I found it in my suitcase, I gave it to the Police Chief. I knew it wasn't mine to keep. Did you put that in my suitcase?"

Colin groaned, ignoring her question.

"I'm dead," he moaned. "I am so dead. She said she would kill me slowly and painfully if I didn't get that necklace back to her. I've been searching for you for weeks. I hid it in the suitcase because I was going to come back to get it when you went to work. I didn't know you were going to half-kill me and then run."

"Don't blame me for the bad decisions you made."

Rachel eyed Colin scornfully. Marcus Taylor's nephew was a thief who was now trying to blame his woes on her.

"Just as you've been forgiven, so you must forgive others."

Her pastor's voice rang in her head. Last week's sermon was now very real. Rachel realized this was someone Christ died for. God had forgiven her and shown her mercy. Now she had to choose if she would do the same for Colin Taylor.

"Mr. Taylor," she began gently. "Colin, I can see you're in some kind of trouble. Come with me to the police. Maggie, the chief, can help you."

"No!"

Colin glanced around nervously, then looked back at Rachel.

"No, I can't go to the police. They'll throw me in jail."

"You won't have to worry about jail, little man. Jacquelyn will kill you long before then. Or maybe I'll do it now."

The deep voice surprised Colin and Rachel. When they turned to see the source, a tall muscular man stood in the nearby alley grinning with an evil gleam in his eyes. He reached out a massive hand and grabbed Colin by the collar, then spun and rammed Colin head first into the brick wall of the first building that lined the alley. He then dropped Colin on the ground, grinning at the sight of Colin as he lay in a broken heap, bleeding profusely.

Satisfied with his work, the big man turned toward Rachel, a leering grin on his face.

"Now, what shall I do with you, sweet thing?"

Rachel knew the look in his eyes. She had seen it in

Colin's eyes the night she thought she'd killed him. Slowly she lowered her purse and shopping bag to the ground and used her foot to push them out of the way. Rachel began to take slow deep breaths as she considered her adversary.

"Remember, size isn't everything."

She could hear her Uncle Jon's voice.

"Use your adversary's size against him. Use your skills to defend yourself until you are sure the danger is past. You have the right to defend yourself, but once the danger is past, you must stop."

Now it was Esther's voice Rachel heard in memory.

The big man sneered at her.

"Just what do you think you're gonna do? You think you can take me on? Ha! I'm gonna have a little fun with you, and who knows, you might even enjoy it."

He took a step toward her, his meaty hands reaching.

"I don't care if you like it or not."

Rachel didn't answer him. She just waited for him to make the first move. When he moved closer to grab her, she grabbed his arm and punched him in the solar plexus. Then she dropped and swept her leg behind his knees. With a look of shock, the man went down on his back.

She heard a cheer behind her. Rachel turned and saw Jason standing at the entrance to the alley. He gave her a big thumbs-up as he approached.

"Jason! What are you doing here? Did you see what happened?"

The young cowhand ignored her questions as he pointed behind her.

"Great job! But look, he's getting away! Should we chase him?"

Rachel turned and saw the big man stumbling down the alley, holding his stomach. She saw Maggie and two police officers, with guns drawn, running toward the alley and calling out for the big man to halt. He sent a venomous glare back at Rachel as he scrambled over the fence.

Jason stepped closer to Rachel, putting out a hand as if to provide comfort or assistance. Rachel turned back to him with a question in her eyes. He nodded.

"I called the police. I tried to get here in time to help, but he had already hurt your friend and then you took care of the big guy."

Now that the danger was past, Rachel was able to turn her attention to Colin. He was still lying motionless on the street. Maggie knelt to check on him, then radioed for an ambulance.

Rachel felt the adrenaline drain from her limbs. She leaned unsteadily against a wall. Maggie walked over and touched her shoulder.

"Are you okay?"

Rachel nodded, though she was actually feeling like she might burst into tears at any moment.

"I'm impressed with your skills."

Maggie eyed her for a moment.

"You've done this before, haven't you?"

Rachel gave her a small smile.

"Yeah, my father and my uncle taught me martial arts as I was growing up. I've been working with Esther to continue my training."

Rachel turned to see a local doctor kneeling beside Colin. Maggie looked that way too.

"Do you know who these men are?"

"I don't know who the big man is. The one that's hurt is Colin Taylor."

Maggie was startled.

"The man you said you killed?"

"Yes, and also the man who put that necklace in my suitcase. Somehow he found me at the ranch."

"I imagine you were not happy to see him."

"Well, I can't say I'm happy to see him; but I am immensely relieved that I didn't kill him."

Rachel stopped to think. She looked at the wounded man with compassion.

"He's been begging me to talk to him. When I came out of the bookstore, he was waiting for me. He seems scared to death of the woman he stole the necklace from. If that big man works for her, I can see why."

Maggie glanced at Colin then back at Rachel and nodded.

"I have an idea or two about that."

"Jason, can you take her back to the Rocking K?"

Jason shook his head.

"I'm sorry, Chief, I can't right now. I have to meet with my counselor. I'm late already."

At Maggie's expression, he hastened to explain.

"I saw what happened. I already gave my statement while you talked to Rachel."

Maggie nodded and turned back to Rachel.

"Let's get your statement and then I'll get an officer to take you back to the Rocking K. You're still in shock and shouldn't drive right now."

When Rachel started to protest about leaving her truck, Maggie waved her off.

"Don't worry, I can bring your truck to you this evening. As soon as Mr. Taylor is able to talk, I want to have a discussion with him about that necklace."

Rachel nodded wearily and, after retrieving her purse and bag, trudged to the squad car, grateful she didn't have to focus on driving. She wondered what Maggie's idea was.

Jacquelyn's cold voice over the phone filled Brock with dread.

"Didn't I tell you that I wanted to kill Colin Taylor myself? Why did you disobey my orders? Your brash actions may have destroyed everything."

Brock heard Jacquelyn's controlled words and tone, but knew her control did not mean she was not angry. He could almost see the glint in her icy blue eyes. He rushed his explanation, the words tumbling out almost faster than he could say them.

"She was trying to persuade him to go to the police. He said no, but I could see he was weakening."

"So instead you drew attention to yourself as well as to Colin and the woman. Then you let the woman take you down."

Brock's pride still stung from being taken down by the young woman he had expected to have a little fun with, and toss aside as he had many others. Then he remembered what the young woman had told Colin when he asked for the necklace.

"I have some useful information for you, though."

Silence met his words for a moment.

"What information?"

"When Taylor accosted the woman and asked her for the necklace, she told him she didn't have it; that she had given it to the police."

Brock heard Jacquelyn swear as she smacked her palm down on the desk. The sound startled him. This woman was always so calm and self-contained that it seemed that nothing startled or surprised her; nothing made her lose that icy self-control. To hear her express anger was frightening to the big man. It meant something was seriously wrong.

There was silence again as the businesswoman calmed herself and tapped her lacquered fingernails on the desktop. The irritating sound meant Jacquelyn was deep in thought. Just when Brock thought he could not stand the noise anymore, his boss spoke.

"That information is indeed useful, but alarming. We need to move on this immediately. I will arrive tomorrow. You will need to stay in hiding until I call you."

Brock started to object, but Jacquelyn interrupted him.

"I will take care of Mr. Taylor myself. His usefulness has come to an end now that we know where the woman and the necklace are. I want you to break into the jail and find that necklace. You will probably find it in the chief's office, so look there first. Do you think you can carry this off without drawing further attention to yourself?"

Brock flushed at the sneer in her voice. He had broken into many places, including police station offices, without ever being caught. Her doubt in his abilities rankled.

"I can do it," he replied sullenly.

"Take care of that tonight. And, Brock?"

He waited, wondering what was next.

"Don't fail me again."

Chapter Fourteen

Jesse tossed the hay bale to another cowboy, then stopped to mop his face with his arm. He and three other hands had been stacking hay bales for a couple hours in the Louisiana heat and humidity. Jesse was drenched with sweat and itching from the little bits of hay that stuck to him.

He wondered what Rachel was doing now. He had seen her drive her "rust bucket" into town earlier. Although he liked to tease her about the old truck, Jesse was actually concerned whenever she drove it. The vehicle had definitely seen better days and Jesse was afraid that it would die on her half-way to town. It would be a long hot walk to town or back to the ranch.

Jesse smiled thinking about his friend. Since he had led Rachel to Christ, the two of them had become close friends. Often Jesse would think he would like to take their relationship in a different direction. He had wondered what it would be like to hold and kiss her. Yet, he felt his past would cast a shadow on any kind of romantic relationship.

"Hey, Dream Boy! I'm waiting for that hay bale!"

Jesse shook himself out of his reverie and reached for the next bale.

"Look! Rachel's coming home in a police car!"

Jesse looked over toward the driveway in time to see Rachel get out of the front seat of the squad car. Concerned by the pallor on her face, he climbed down from the pile of hay bales and strode toward her. He wondered if her truck had finally died. That would account for the police officer bringing her home.

When he got closer to Rachel, he saw the fear and grief on her face. This was no issue with a broken-down truck. He held open his arms and she ran to him and buried her face in his shirt. Sobs shook her slender form as he cradled her gently against him.

"Rachel, what's wrong, honey?"

Jesse didn't even notice the endearment he had just used. He was worried about Rachel.

"Hey," he lifted her head and tilted her chin so he could meet her tear-drenched eyes. "Come on, tell me what happened."

"Ms. James, Maggie wanted me to tell you that she'll bring your truck to you after she gets done at the hospital."

Jesse was alarmed as Rachel nodded her understanding. Hospital? What was going on?

As the squad car drove toward the gate, Jesse squeezed Rachel's shoulders with the arm he had kept draped around her. He could feel the tension and exhaustion radiating through her. Just as he opened his mouth to ask her what was going on, Kendall approached.

"Rachel, what happened? Why did the police bring you home? Are you all right?"

Jesse dropped his arm from Rachel's shoulders and motioned to Kendall that he wanted to talk to her. He gave Rachel a reassuring smile, then moved a few steps away to confer with his boss.

"I'm not sure, but I think something happened while

she was in town," he said in a low tone. "I was just about to talk to her about it."

Kendall searched his eyes. Apparently satisfied with what she saw there, she nodded.

"I'll get with you later then. Rachel, you let me know if you need something, hear?"

With that she hurried toward the barn, shouting at the other hands to get back to work.

Jesse stepped to Rachel's side and walked her to her cabin. Once inside, he took her purse and set it on the kitchen counter. Then he sat on the couch and pulled her down beside him.

"Okay, tell me what happened. You look shell-shocked."

"Jesse, Colin came up and asked to talk to me when I came out of the bookstore. While we were talking, this big man came up. He grabbed Colin and rammed his head into the concrete. Then he tried to attack me. I took him down. Jason was there and called the police, but the attacker got up and ran away when the police arrived."

Rachel was crying again as she tried to tell her story. Jesse was angry that Colin had accosted her again and bothered her about that necklace. He wondered why the self-assured wealthy man was so afraid of the mysterious woman. But when Rachel described the attack, Jesse felt a surge of protective rage.

This sweet woman had been attacked first by Colin Taylor and now by this stranger. Jesse felt like he wanted to punch someone. No, he wanted to punch Colin Taylor and the big man that had so frightened Rachel.

He turned to the woman next to him and ran his hand over her hair. Lately he had been noticing auburn highlights and thought they were beautiful on her. He pulled her close to him as she again soaked his shirt. Jesse felt a warmth inside that she trusted him enough to cry on his shoulder and that she didn't even seem to notice how sweaty and dirty he was.

He held Rachel gently as he continued to run his hand down her hair and spoke in soothing tones.

"I'm so proud of you for taking that bully down. But it scares the daylights out of me to think of what he could have done to you. If anything happened to you, I don't know what I'd do."

Rachel pulled back and stared into his warm brown eyes. He returned the gaze, his hand moving of its own volition to trace her cheek. Something stirred within him that filled him with tenderness for this brave and beautiful young woman. Slowly his face moved toward her as he cupped her head in his hand.

She didn't move away. In fact, Rachel leaned forward, her lips parted slightly. He leaned forward and gently claimed those sweet lips. She returned the kiss, sliding her arms around his neck and moving closer. Suddenly Jesse came to himself. What was he doing? Rachel deserved better than him. He backed away, reluctantly ending the kiss.

"I'm sorry, Rachel. I shouldn't have taken advantage of you like that."

Rachel's eyes registered confusion.

"You didn't take advantage of me, Jesse. I liked kissing you."

Jesse wouldn't look at her. He was falling hard for Rachel, but he felt he didn't deserve such a sweet and gentle woman. He surged to his feet and turned to look at her. She was so pretty. She also looked like she was getting mad. He took a step toward the door.

"Hold it buster."

Rachel was standing behind him now.

"I think you better tell me what's going on here."

She softened her tone.

"Jesse, I'm starting to feel something more than friendship for you. I think you feel it too. Why are you running from me?"

He looked back at her; his eyes troubled.

"I do feel something for you, Rachel. But you know my history. I'm a former drug dealer. I'm not good enough for you and never will be."

Rachel grabbed his arm, her expression hurt and angry.

"Didn't you tell me God can forgive anything?"

Jesse hesitated, but Rachel charged ahead.

"You did! When I asked you if that preacher was right, you said he was. You told me that God can forgive any sin. If God can forgive me for killing a man, why can't He forgive you for selling drugs?"

"But you didn't kill him, Rachel."

She waved off his protest.

"When I prayed to accept Jesus as my Lord and Savior I believed I had killed Colin. I almost did. You told me . . ."

Jesse looked down at the hand he had laid on hers, as if startled to see he had touched her again. He sighed and closed his eyes for a moment. When he looked up, his eyes were sad and haunted.

"Yes, God can forgive any sin and I believe He has forgiven me. But I haven't forgiven myself. I can't forgive myself. I can't have any kind of relationship with you with that hanging over me."

With that, Jesse opened her door and strode out into the afternoon sun. Rachel watched him walk away. She laid her hand on her lips, remembering their kiss.

"Oh, Jesse," Rachel murmured. "You have to forgive yourself some time."

"Hey Spence, have you seen Kendall? I need to ask her about something."

Jesse leaned against the post on the corral and watched as Spence worked with a young gelding. He noticed how patient the older cowboy was with the animal; gently correcting instead of yelling or losing his temper when the horse wouldn't go the way Spence wanted. That was one of the things Jesse appreciated about the older man. He was quiet and patient, always willing to help but never butting in. Kind of like Rachel. She was sweet and patient.

"Young man, did you even hear me?"

Jesse started. He realized Spence had been answering him while his thoughts had wandered.

"Sorry, Spence. I wasn't paying attention. Too much on my mind, I guess."

Spence slid off of the gelding and tied its reins loosely on the post. He turned toward Jesse and eyed him closely.

"You thinking about that sweet gal that cooks our meals?"

Jesse just gave a short nod and turned as if to look for Kendall.

"You two seem to have something special. I'd think that would make you happy. But you look as if you're carrying some kind of heavy load."

The younger man turned around to look Spence in the eye. They stood looking at each other in silence for a moment, then Jesse slumped.

"Rachel is special and much too good for someone like me."

"How's that?"

Spence took a package of gum out of his pocket and slid a piece into his mouth. He offered it silently to Jesse who shook his head.

When Jesse didn't answer, the cowboy watched him for a moment, then laid a hand on his shoulder.

"Boy, I've been watching you ever since you came to the Rocking K. You were a scared defiant kid when you got here. Expected everyone to hold against you the fact that you sold drugs."

When Jesse started to object Spence stopped him.

"Just hold on and let me say my piece. Then I'll leave you alone. You've grown into a fine, godly young man and I'm proud to know you."

Jesse mumbled an embarrassed thanks.

"But you got to forgive yourself, Jesse, just like God's forgiven you. You got to stop expecting folks to think the worst of you and move on. Your drug dealing days are way behind you now. If you keep looking back, you'll miss the bright future God has for you. Let go of it, young man, and look ahead."

Spence untied the gelding and swung into the saddle. "I've said what I have to say. Just think about it."

Jesse sat quietly at the table with the other cowhands as they enjoyed another one of Rachel's delicious dinners. Appreciative sounds filled the air as the cowhands devoured the peach cobbler and ice cream. For most of the hungry men, the ice cream didn't even have time to melt on the hot cobbler before the dessert was finished and bowls held up for seconds.

"Hey, Jess, aren't you going to eat your dessert? That's some prime peach cobbler right there."

Jesse gave a small grin to the cowboy next to him.

"You can't have my cobbler, Jim. I'm about to dig into it. Just have a lot to think about."

"With good cooking like Miss Rachel's, I'd be thinking about my food."

To look at Jim's thin and wiry frame, you'd swear he never ate anything. But the man could eat anyone else under the table.

Rachel waited until the other cowhands got up from their meal, then bent over to speak in Jesse's ear.

"Meet me outside at the corral in about an hour, okay? I need to talk to you."

She was afraid that after the way he'd left her cabin, Jesse would refuse. But he nodded without looking at her.

Rachel hurried to clear the table and get the dishes washed. As she wiped the counters, she thought again about what she wanted to say to Jesse.

When she stepped outside, Rachel saw Jesse standing by the corral, stroking the nose of one of the mares. She couldn't help smiling at the scene. Rachel felt a thrill run through her as she watched him talking to the horse and petting it. He was such a patient and gentle man. If only he would be that patient with himself.

Jesse could sense her presence when Rachel walked toward him. He looked up from the horse to watch her. Rachel moved with a gentle grace that only added to her beauty. He saw her stop to pet her dog, Angel who came trotting up for a scratch behind the ears.

After the way he'd acted in her cabin, he wouldn't blame her if she laid into him and then never had anything to do with him again.

Rachel stopped a couple feet away and squeezed her hands in front of her. She fumbled in her pocket for Angel's ball and threw it for the Border Collie to retrieve. Jesse realized she was nervous around him. He felt a pang of guilt for the damage he knew he had caused to their friendship.

When she spoke, her rapid rush of words surprised him.

"Jesse, I want you to know that I care a lot about you. If you feel the same way I do, I'd be willing to see where our relationship can go. If you don't want anything more than friendship, then I'll be your friend."

She stopped to take the ball from Angel and throw it again. Before Jesse could answer, however, Rachel's old truck came bouncing down the driveway, with a squad car right behind it. It came to a stop in front of the house.

Rachel started toward the truck as Maggie stepped out of it. Jesse and Angel followed close behind her. As she drew near the police chief, she could see Maggie wore a grim expression.

"Maggie, thank you for bringing my truck. Would you like to come in for some peach cobbler?"

"You're welcome, Rachel. Yes, I would love some of your peach cobbler. I've heard some of the cowhands from here bragging about your cooking. They say you could open your own bakery."

Rachel extended the offer to the young officer as he got out of the squad car, but he declined. Maggie stepped to his side and spoke with him briefly in a low tone. The officer nodded and leaned against the car.

Maggie returned to Rachel's truck and eased the truck door closed. She turned to Rachel and Jesse, who fell into step beside her. Rachel sent Angel to lay in front of her cabin door.

"Did you tell Jesse what happened when you were in town?"

Rachel nodded and Jesse laid his hand on her shoulder.

Maggie gestured toward the house.

"Let's go in and I'll give you an update on what I've learned so far."

Once inside, Rachel hurried to warm up some coffee and dish up a serving of the dessert for Maggie. The police chief dug into her bowl of cobbler and washed the first few bites down with swallows of Rachel's special-blend coffee. Then she wiped her mouth and looked across the table at Rachel's pale face.

"First, I have to tell you the bad news. The man who attacked you and Mr. Taylor got away. My officers chased him for a couple of blocks, but he managed to slip away from them."

Rachel remembered the evil leer in the assailant's eyes. Since she had seen his face, she realized, he could come after her again. A shudder ran through her.

"Second, Mr. Taylor has been airlifted to a Shreveport hospital. I visited the ICU where they've admitted him. He has a severe concussion and is in pretty bad shape, but the doctor seems to think he'll make it. He'll have a long recovery, though. There's a twenty-four-hour guard on him. If he wakes up, we want to hear what he has to say.

Jesse leaned forward.

"What else, Maggie? You look like you have something else on your mind."

Maggie grinned at him.

"Very perceptive, Jess. Yes, there is something more."

She went on to tell them about the flash drive her son had found and the business information that was on that drive. Maggie told about her friend at the FBI.

"Monica thinks the woman Mr. Taylor stole the necklace from, Jacquelyn Marquette, is the same person the FBI has been investigating for industrial espionage. That flash drive may have provided some key evidence in their case."

"Rachel, you need to be extra careful. Your attacker is still at large. We think Ms. Marquette may be the one who employs him. She's also known to be a cold-blooded killer. There's never been enough evidence to arrest her, but that may change in the near future."

Jesse slid closer to Rachel as if to protect her. Maggie noticed the gesture.

"I can't emphasize enough how much you need to be watchful. I wish I could assign some of my officers to guard you, but I just don't have the manpower."

"There's no need for that."

The trio at the table turned at the sound of Kendall's voice.

"My hands will protect Rachel. I'll make sure each of them is armed and that at least one of them is with her at all times."

Maggie stood to shake hands with the ranch owner.

"Kendall, I appreciate the sentiment, but I don't want you or your employees taking the law into your own hands. Also, keep in mind that several of your hands are on parole or probation. Giving them firearms is not a good idea."

"We're not vigilantes, Maggie. But we like to protect our own."

Maggie nodded.

"Understood. All of you, please be careful."

Rachel felt a tremor run through her. Even with the offer of protection, it seemed as if evil was reaching out to grab her. As his comforting arm squeezed her shoulders, she turned to see Jesse's tender brown eyes.

"Don't worry, Rachel. We're here for you. *I'm* here for you."

Chapter Fifteen

Brock slid his knife into his pocket and eased open the window to the police chief's office. Because of the late hour, no one was around in downtown Forrestville. There were a couple of lights on in the police station, but not in the chief's office.

The intruder grinned as he stepped through the window and silently slid it almost shut. He stopped to let his eyes adjust to the dim lighting in the room, then began a systematic search of the desk.

Finally, he opened a small drawer and found a velvet pouch. Brock felt a jolt of adrenaline as he peeked inside the pouch and saw the gleam of gold and red enamel. He poured the necklace into his hand to make sure he had the right item. Confirming his find, he slid it back into the pouch and tucked the pouch in his pocket. He closed the drawer and turned toward the window.

Brock paused, feeling like he was forgetting something. He had to make sure he did this right. He felt the outline of the pendant in his pocket and nodded. He had what Jacquelyn wanted. Now he could get back in her good graces.

He slid the window open and squirmed through, landing quietly on the grass outside. Then he turned and blended into the shadows.

After he had disappeared down the street, a form appeared in the window, back lit by a small lamp on the desk. Maggie smiled grimly as she opened the drawer where she had "hidden" the pendant. She picked up her office phone and dialed.

"He picked it up tonight," she told her friend on the other end.

"Do you think they'll notice the little gift we left?"

Maggie grinned.

"Time will tell."

"Jacquelyn, I mean, Ms. Marquette, I have it. I have the necklace!"

The door to the hotel room cracked open and the businesswoman peered out. Satisfied that he was alone, she opened the door and waved him in.

Jacquelyn was staying in a hotel in Shreveport so that she could meet with her right-hand man away from prying eyes. Now she reached for the object in his hands, avarice gleaming in her eyes.

Brock eagerly handed the velvet pouch to his employer, trying not to wince when her long nails scratched his hand as she snatched the prize from him.

Jacquelyn opened the pouch and poured the pendant with its long gold chain into her hand. She admired the bright stones set in the gold and red.

"Good job, Brock. I knew you could pull it off."

Brock knew better than to bask for too long in her praise. She could change from praise to invectives in an instant, all without losing her cool.

Jacquelyn turned the pendant over to open the back. Her eyes widened in shock when she saw it was empty, no flash drive. She turned the ladybug over and searched it intently. When she realized there was no flash drive in the pendant, she tossed it on her desk, her ice blue eyes flashing in anger. Something caught her eye, and she snatched the ladybug up again.

Narrowing her eyes, Jacquelyn peered inside the cavity that had held the flash drive. She reached in the desk drawer and brought out a pair of tweezers.

A moment later she held up a tiny black object which she laid on the desk and covered with a folded scarf.

She tapped the desk with her long fingernails, the sound becoming increasingly rapid and repetitive in her agitation. Brock had never seen Jacquelyn like this. She always maintained a calm, cool appearance. But now his boss was angry and frustrated. He knew she was going to lay into him before she even started.

"You imbecile!" she ground out. "I gave you a simple job to do and you have failed me again."

"I, I don't understand," he stuttered. "I brought you the necklace. Isn't that what you wanted?"

"I don't need this shiny bauble! I need the flash drive I had inside of it. Instead you bring me an FBI tracker."

She shook her head at his look of disbelief.

"Yes, FBI. A small-town police station wouldn't have technology like this."

Jacquelyn picked up the necklace and threw it at her henchman.

"Did you check inside it like I told you? Never mind answering. I know you didn't. You forgot or you were interrupted, or some other lame excuse. Don't even try to defend yourself."

She came around the desk and slapped him. Brock reeled back. He felt anger bubble inside him. He had faithfully served her ever since she bailed him out of jail more than ten years prior. He had done whatever she wanted, whenever she wanted, in just the way she wanted. But in the past year she had started to verbally abuse him and inflict painful little punishments whenever things didn't go her way.

Jacquelyn looked into his eyes, her cold stare cutting through his anger and igniting fear. Brock knew she was very good at hurting and killing, then hiding the evidence. If she decided she didn't need him anymore, he would be dead before the end of the day and she would find a new right-hand man.

"I can see I can't count on you, Brock. I will have to decide what that means later. Right now I need to visit poor Mr. Taylor in the hospital and make sure he doesn't share any information."

Brock stood and watched Jacquelyn in silence. He wasn't sure what he should do at this point. His boss looked at him with contempt.

"Don't worry, Brock. I won't kill you, for now. You've been a good worker in the past, so I might decide to keep you. In fact, I'll give you another assignment. Try not to mess this one up. Watch Ms. James. When she leaves the ranch, find a way to sabotage her vehicle. I want her stranded for a while so that you can search her cabin. It may be she either found the flash drive or it fell out while the pendant was in her possession. If you find the drive, you will be back in my good graces. If you don't, well, we'll see what happens then."

She lifted the scarf and picked up the tracker, which she handed to Brock.

"Drop this in someone's car. Maybe we can distract the FBI while we take care of business."

Jacquelyn admired the hospital name tag. If she hadn't watched the man create it in front of her, she wouldn't have recognized it as hers. The blond hair and green eyes completely transformed her.

"I like it."

"That will be $150."

The young man who made his illegal living creating false ID's didn't waste time on chitchat. He simply listened to what the client wanted, created it, and collected his money. He didn't ask for real names and he only gave them his street name - Pic.

Jacquelyn peeled off two $100 bills.

"I like to reward good work," she explained when Pic quirked an eyebrow at her. He grunted and stuffed the money in his pocket.

Next Jacquelyn went shopping. She visited a specialty store and picked out a set of blue scrubs and a pair of clogs. Her final stop was a florist shop, where she selected flowers for a small bouquet.

"They're for a sick friend of mine," she told the cashier as she paid. The cashier nodded and smiled.

Jacquelyn gave her a sweet smile as she left.

"Have a nice day!"

Leaving the floral shop, Jacquelyn placed the bouquet in a box she had brought for transporting it. Then she pulled out a small vial and a needle. Carefully she filled the hypodermic and capped it, sliding it into her pocket.

"Now to go wish Mr. Taylor a nice day."

Chapter Sixteen

"Kendall, I'm ready when you are."

Rachel gathered her purse and a cold bottle of water for the ride into town. She and Kendall were doing the shopping today since Kendall said she needed a break from the ranch. Rachel had some personal shopping to do, then she needed to pick up groceries and supplies for the ranch kitchen.

Jesse spotted her as she moved toward her old truck.

"Rachel, I thought you were riding with Kendall."

His worried tone touched Rachel. He had been protective but a little distant recently.

"I'll be fine," she answered. "I need the truck for the supplies. Kendall needs her truck for the sacks of feed. Don't worry, I'm following her to and from town."

She could see Jesse still didn't like it. Although his concern for her was nice, she felt a bit resentful too. Didn't he think she could take care of herself? After all, she had taken down the big man who attacked Colin.

Of course, she had fallen apart when she got back to the ranch that day. Rachel sighed. It seemed whenever something happened, she turned into a soggy mess that Jesse had to hold and comfort. No wonder he didn't think she could take care of herself.

Kendall came out of the house and headed toward her truck. Jesse caught up with her and had a low conversation with his boss, sweeping his gaze toward Rachel every now and then. Kendall just shook her head and motioned for him to go back to work.

"Jesse, we're big girls. I think we can handle a trip to town and back. I need you here to finish those chores."

The two women got in their vehicles and drove down the highway to Forrestville. When they entered the small town, they found parking for both trucks near the diner. Rachel had to laugh as Kendall made a big show of locking her truck doors and checking them, then making sure Rachel did the same.

Rachel tucked her purse close as she swept the street with her eyes. Since the attack on her and Colin, she had tried to stay extra vigilant. She spotted the sign for the Christian bookstore and turned to her companion.

"Kendall, I just need a minute in here. I want to see those scarves you were talking about and spend some of the gift card you gave me.

"That's fine. I like looking around in the bookstore. I may do a little spending myself. There are a couple of CD's and DVD's I wanted to look for. Don't rush, we have plenty of time."

Rachel found the rack of scarves, but was a bit overwhelmed at the selection. She had not expected to find so many scarves that seemed perfect for her. It was hard to narrow it down.

Kendall stood behind her and watched her pick up a scarf, then set it down and pick up another one. A glint of gold on a red scarf caught her eye. She reached for the scarf and smiled when she saw "I Love Jesus" scattered over the silky material. Kendall held it up for Rachel to see.

"I think this one is perfect for you, Rachel. That shade of red looks good on you and see what the gold lettering says? That's what everyone can see in you now."

Rachel blushed at the compliment and took the scarf to look at it. She wrapped it around her neck and glanced in a nearby mirror. Her eyes shining, she nodded at Kendall.

"Thank you, Kendall. I appreciate the encouragement. You're right; this scarf is perfect for me. I'll get this and the Armor of God pin that I found. Then we can head over to get the groceries."

After paying for her purchases, Rachel picked up her bag and headed out the door with Kendall right behind her. As she stepped outside, Rachel felt the hairs on the back of her neck stand up. She felt as if someone was watching her. She stopped and stared around her, trying to pinpoint where the feeling was coming from.

Kendall laid her hand on Rachel's shoulder.

"You okay?"

"Yeah," she answered slowly. "Just, a feeling."

She shook her head and smiled at her boss.

"I guess I'm just super sensitive right now."

Kendall looked worried.

"Are you sure?"

Rachel nodded and motioned across the street. She didn't want their day in town ruined by Kendall worrying about her.

"I'll see you after we finish our respective shopping."

Kendall didn't look convinced, but took Rachel's word that she was okay and headed off to take care of her errands. Rachel took another look around. She still couldn't see anything, but she could *feel* it.

The feeling stayed with her until Rachel got to the supermarket. Then she was too busy trying to find everything on her list. Kendall and Rachel planned to meet at their trucks when they were done.

Rachel finally got everything on her list and made it to the checkout. She chatted with the cashier as everything was rung up and paid for. Then she tucked her wallet in her purse and walked out to the truck. When she left the market, Rachel stopped and swept the street with her eyes again. She didn't see anything that alarmed her and the feeling of being watched was gone.

The stock boy who helped her load the items into her truck wasn't as friendly as the cashier. He simply pushed the buggy to the truck and hefted the groceries into the back. Rachel smiled and thanked him anyway as she handed him a few dollars for a tip. He grunted what passed for thanks and strode away, the buggy rattling as he pushed it across the parking lot and into the store.

Kendall came around her truck with a worried look, her cell phone in hand. Rachel noticed that the lines around Kendall's eyes had deepened and her mouth was set in a grim line.

"What's wrong?"

"Jesse just called me. One of the hands, Andy, fell in the barn. They don't know the full extent of his injuries yet, but it looks bad. He may need surgery tonight. I need to go to Forrestville General to meet the ambulance. Will you be okay driving back alone?"

Rachel waved her away.

"I'll be fine. I drove all the way here from Texas by myself."

She persuaded Kendall to go on to the hospital while she took the groceries back to the ranch.

"Don't worry. I'll be especially careful. I'll drive straight back to the ranch. Go on. You need to be there for Andy."

Kendall finally got in her truck to go to the hospital. Rachel got into hers and stopped to say a little prayer for Andy. Then she started the truck and backed out of the spot, turning onto the main highway. She was so intent on getting back to the ranch that she did not notice the spot of gasoline left in her parking place, or the small trail that her truck left as it puttered down the road.

Rachel turned on the radio and sang along as she drove. Then something on the dash caught her eye. Her gas tank was almost empty! How did that happen? She had filled up just a couple days ago. The drive to town wasn't that long.

The old truck coughed and died. Rachel steered the truck to the side of the road and put it in Park. She pulled out her cell phone and was dismayed to see that she had no signal in this area at all. Now that she thought about it she remembered Jesse commenting that this was a dead zone for cell phones.

Rachel got out and stood looking up and down the highway. At this time of day the traffic was pretty light. She sighed and reached back into the truck for her purse and the fresh bottle of water she had bought when she checked out at the market. It looked like she was going to have to walk home.

"I'm glad I don't have anything perishable," Rachel muttered. "At least I don't have to worry about food spoiling. I'll just have to walk back to the ranch and get someone to come get the supplies."

The first couple of miles were fairly easy, but Rachel's water began to get low about the time her energy started to flag. The temperature that day was in the mid-90's with high humidity. Rachel began to feel a little nauseated and light-headed. She walked to a nearby tree and leaned against it, trying to get cool in the sparse amount of shade provided.

"I can't give in to this," she prodded herself. "I'll rest here a minute, then see if I can go another mile before I rest again."

The words were barely out of her mouth when she heard a shout from the road. Shading her eyes, Rachel looked toward the highway and saw a beautiful sight. Willie was standing next to his tow truck which was pulled onto the shoulder.

"Ms. James, what are you doing out here in this heat?" The mechanic wore a worried expression.

"I saw your truck back there. What happened?"

Rachel gratefully accepted Willie's help into the tow truck and aimed the air vents at her face. Her rescuer rummaged in a small cooler and handed her a bottle of water.

"Drink it slow, now," he cautioned.

Rachel nodded and sipped the cool liquid.

"I'm not sure what happened with my truck," she finally answered. "I filled up a couple days ago and haven't really done much driving. But on the way back from town I noticed my gas gauge was at Empty. The poor old truck just coughed and died."

Willie nodded thoughtfully.

"You know, I thought I saw a puddle of gas in your parking place when you pulled out. Let me put a couple gallons in for you and follow you back to the ranch. I can check it there."

When Rachel protested she didn't want to be any trouble, Willie waved her off.

"It's no trouble, missy. I'm glad to help. I'd sure hate for you to get hurt or sick walking out in this hot weather."

Willie turned the tow truck around and they arrived at her truck in just a few minutes. Rachel stayed in the tow truck while Willie poured gasoline into her truck. When he waved to her, she reluctantly left the coolness of the tow truck and moved to his side.

"Thank you, Willie! You are a guardian angel."

Willie beamed back at her.

"Now you drive careful. I'll follow you back to the Rocking K. I needed to make a trip there anyway to ask Spence about something."

Rachel hopped into her truck and rolled her window down. With only a couple of gallons of gas, she didn't want to add any extra work to the engine, so she left the air conditioner off. Willie nodded his approval as he pulled his truck behind her and followed her home. Rachel lifted up a short prayer.

"Thank You, God, for sending Willie. Please get me back to the ranch safely. Thank You for always watching out for me."

When Rachel and Willie turned into the gate at the Rocking K, Jesse came out of the barn. Rachel waved to him, then frowned as she saw the thunderous look on his face.

"Why are you driving alone? I thought you were with Kendall! You promised you would stay with her! What's going on?"

Rachel felt her temper rising, but managed to answer him coolly.

"Kendall went to the hospital. I decided to drive back to the ranch so I could put the supplies away."

"Then what took you so long?"

Now Rachel was getting mad. He was acting as if he was her boss.

"For your information, Mr. Bossy, my truck ran out of gas. I was walking back when Willie came along and helped me."

Too late Rachel realized she was confirming his earlier fears about her driving the old pickup. She looked him straight in the eye. He might as well know the worst of it.

"Willie thinks something is wrong with the fuel line."

Jesse glanced at Rachel's truck where Willie was stretched out underneath. When he looked back at Rachel, she glared at him.

"Don't you even think about saying something snarky about my truck, Jesse Williams!"

She whirled and stomped over to the little pickup. Jesse hesitated, then followed her. Willie squeezed out from under the truck and joined them. He wiped his hands on a dirty handkerchief.

"Ms. James, I can't tell for sure without putting it up on my rack, but I think someone messed with your fuel line."

Rachel swayed. Jesse stepped forward and wrapped his arm around her waist.

"Are . . . are you sure?"

"No, ma'am, not one hundred percent, but what I could see under there sure looked like it."

Jesse guided her to the back of the truck and lowered the tailgate. He eased her up so that she could sit and stood in front of her, a worried expression replacing the angry frown he had worn just a few minutes earlier.

Willie pulled him aside. Rachel could hear his low tone as he filled Jesse in.

"Jesse, I found that little lady about three miles from her truck. She was walking in the heat. I got her into my truck and turned up the A/C, but I think she's been through a lot this afternoon."

Jesse thanked the mechanic and reassured him that Rachel would be well cared-for. Rachel stood and thanked Willie for his help. After her rescuer was gone, Rachel turned to Jesse, trying to look stronger than she felt.

"I'm really much better, now. It just came as a shock, knowing someone tampered with my fuel line. I don't know who would do that, or why."

Her voice tapered off as her eyes met Jesse's intense gaze. Horror swept through her.

"You think the man who attacked Colin did this?"

Jesse wrapped his arm around her waist again as he directed her toward the main house.

"Remember, he tried to attack you too. He may have wanted to get you off alone."

"But if that was it, why didn't he attack me while I was walking? I was out there a long time without anyone around."

Jesse thought about it as they walked inside the house. He steered Rachel toward the living room and made her sit on the couch, giving her a quelling look when she tried to insist she needed to get up and start working on supper.

"You know, Rachel, it might have been some kind of diversion. We'll call Maggie after you've had time to cool off and rest."

Rachel laid her head back on the couch, enjoying the cool breeze from the ceiling fan.

"Okay. After I cool off, can you help me unload the supplies from my truck? Most of it will go in the pantry, but I have some stuff that needs to go in my cabin."

Jesse nodded.

"That's fine. *After* you rest and cool off."

"Okay, I think I've got a good grip. Can you go ahead and open the door before I drop these?"

Jesse grunted as he lifted the case of soft drinks.

"I don't see why you're not taking these to the main house. They're for everybody, aren't they?"

Rachel's eyes sparkled.

"I'm planning a surprise for the guys next Saturday. Root beer floats! If they see the root beer, either they'll figure out the surprise too early or they'll drink them up before I'm ready."

Rachel hurried to get her key in the door and shove it open.

"Thanks for the help, Jesse."

She moved out of Jesse's way and plopped her bags on the couch. Then she stopped in the middle of the room and looked around in apprehension. Something didn't feel quite right.

Jesse set the case on the kitchen floor and came to stand by Rachel.

"What's wrong?"

Rachel slowly turned in a circle, her eyes narrowing as she examined each corner of her small cabin.

"I don't know. Something just feels different in here. I can't say what, but it just feels different. Like, maybe someone was in here."

Jesse's protective instincts kicked in. He swept the cabin with his own gaze.

"Okay, let's walk through and see if anything is out of place."

The two started toward the kitchen, then paused when they heard a scratch at the door.

"Oh, that must be Angel!"

Rachel hurried to let her dog in.

"Hey, girl! Did you have a good day today? Are you ready for some food and water?"

Angel licked Rachel's face and hands, then turned her head to stare into the bedroom. A low growl emanated from her chest as she stalked through the door. Jesse and Rachel exchanged alarmed expressions and followed the collie, who was sniffing around the chest of drawers and the closet.

Rachel felt a shiver run through her. Angel had just confirmed her fear. Someone had been in her cabin while she was out. For the second time in the past few weeks someone had invaded her space.

Jesse took hold of her elbow and steered her toward the bed.

"You better sit down," he coaxed her. "You look pale and trembly."

Rachel sank down on the bed and stared around her.

"Jesse, what is going on? Why would someone come in here? I don't have anything valuable to steal."

"What about the pendant you found and gave to Maggie?" he suggested. His face was grim as he stood by Rachel.

"We better call Maggie. I think you should ask Kendall to let you and Angel stay in the main house until this is resolved."

Rachel didn't say a word. She just nodded and headed for the door. She didn't want to spend another minute in her cabin.

"You okay?"

Jesse's hand on her shoulder provided a small amount of comfort. He had called Maggie, then ushered Rachel and Angel to the main house. Angel curled up in the mud room and thumped her tail as the cowboys came in for dinner.

Rachel hurried to put a simple meal on the table. She was glad she had assembled a stew in the large crock pot before she and Kendall went to town that morning. Their trip now seemed like it was a long time ago.

Kendall and Jesse stood conversing in low tones in a corner of the dining room. Rachel threw a nervous glance at them every now and then. Finally, she couldn't stand it anymore and moved to join them.

"Kendall, I'm sorry I've been so much trouble. I'll understand if you don't want me to be your cook and housekeeper anymore."

The ranch owner gave her a puzzled look for a moment. Then she laughed as she enveloped Rachel in a hug.When she stepped back, she laid her hands on Rachel's shoulders and gave a gentle shake.

"Oh, no, my dear! We're not letting you go that easily. You're part of the family now. You're stuck with us."

Rachel blinked back tears and gave Kendall a radiant smile. She couldn't believe how quickly this ranch had become a loving home.

"Thank you."

She took off her apron and laid it on the counter.

"I'm not very hungry. I think I'll wait for Maggie outside."

Kendall shot a look at Jesse, who nodded once and walked to the door with Rachel.

"I don't think you should be outside alone. I'm not very hungry either, so I'll come outside with you."

"Jesse, you don't have to babysit me. I'm just going to the front porch."

He gave her a stern look.

"Like I said, I don't think you should be outside alone

right now. Come on, Rachel. We just learned that someone was in your cabin. That person could be hiding anywhere on the ranch."

Jesse looked over his shoulder, into the lighted house. He could hear the hum of conversation at the table as the cowboys dug into the meal.

"If you don't want to stand with me, I can get someone else. Any one of the hands in there would be glad to stand out here to protect you."

Rachel swallowed the lump in her throat and touched Jesse's hand.

"I'd like for you to stay."

She looked down for a moment, trying to hide her heated cheeks. When she looked up again, she found Jesse studying her. Before she could say anything else, Maggie's car swept through the gate and down the long drive.

The two of them hurried down the steps to meet Maggie in the driveway. She motioned toward the cabins.

"Let's go to your cabin. I want you to tell me exactly what you saw, and even felt, when you entered. Also, get Angel. I want to see if she reacts the same way."

Rachel opened the front door and whistled for Angel. They heard the dog's nails on the hardwood floor and saw her nose push through the kitchen door. The collie trotted to the waiting trio and took her place at Rachel's side.

When they got to the cabin, Jesse took the key from Rachel's trembling hand and unlocked the door. Maggie asked Rachel to make Angel wait outside for a few minutes, then stepped inside and moved to a place where she could observe without getting in the way.

"Okay, show and tell me exactly what you did and saw."

Rachel took a deep breath, trying to control the panic that welled up. She described entering the cabin, feeling that something was out of place, and watching Angel's reaction when she entered the cabin.

"Did you *see* anything out of place?"

"Right then, no. It was just a feeling."

"But you see something now?"

Rachel slowly swept the cabin with her gaze, finally stopping at her dresser.

"Yes. My grandmother's teacup is facing the wrong way. The little trinket box has the lid on it. I usually lay the lid next to it. My photographs are switched around. Usually I have the picture of my father and uncle next to my bed and the picture of Angel and me on the dresser. But, I can see now that they're switched."

Maggie slowly paced around the small living space. Finally, she stopped and asked Rachel to bring Angel in.

Rachel opened the door and called her dog. As soon as the collie entered the cabin, she growled and stalked into the bedroom, sniffing and growling around the dresser and bed. With her nose to the floor, the little dog sniffed all through the house, stopping every now and then to growl.

Maggie and Jesse trailed after Rachel as she hurried to the spots where Angel stopped and growled. At each spot, Rachel found more evidence of someone tampering with her belongings.

"It's as if the person put it back *almost* the way I had it."

Maggie shook her head.

"I don't like it," she muttered. "I think someone is trying to play psychological games with you, Rachel. Like he, or she, is trying to frighten you or throw you off balance."

Rachel stared at the small space that had been her home for a couple of months. It had seemed so cozy when she moved in. Now it looked menacing to her.

"Well, it's working. I'm definitely frightened."

Chapter Seventeen

The hospital corridors were mostly empty, with just an occasional nurse or aide walking by in the course of their duties. Jacquelyn waited until the nurse at the desk stepped away in answer to a call from a patient. Then, with a stealthy glance around, she leaned over the counter to search for Colin's room number.

There! She made note of the room number, then carefully picked up the large vase of flowers she was ostensibly bringing to the patient. What Jacquelyn actually planned to bring to him was a quick but agonizing death. Unfortunately, she would not have time to hang around to watch. As soon as she injected the poison into his IV, she would have to leave.

Jacquelyn pasted a sympathetic smile on her face as she carried the flowers to the room on the chart. Her steps slowed as she approached the room. In light of the fact that Colin was attacked, there should be an officer stationed at the door. She noticed the Styrofoam cup with a small amount of coffee in the bottom, as well as a men's bathroom across the hall.

She rolled her eyes.

"These hick police must think I'm a complete idiot to fall for that trap," she muttered.

She quickly concocted a plan, then entered the hospital room, still hoping to inject Colin and get away before anyone noticed.

Jacquelyn paused just inside the room and looked around. The door to the bathroom was closed, but she could see shadows underneath. Her eyes moved to the motionless form in the bed. She glanced at his hand and wrist that. No scratches!

She wanted to throw something. Colin wasn't even in the room! She set the flowers down and fingered the syringe in her pocket. Jacquelyn was tempted to inject the figure on the bed just because he was part of ruining her plan.

She abandoned that idea when she heard the bathroom door open. Jacquelyn began fussing with the flowers in the arrangement.

"What are you doing in here?"

At the harsh voice Jacquelyn jumped and backed away a step. Holding her hand over her heart, she widened her eyes.

"I was told to bring these flowers to this room."

"You're not supposed to be in here. How did you get in? Let me see some identification"

"I just walked in. I'm a nurse here."

Jacquelyn turned a frightened, innocent gaze on the officers as she showed them her hospital badge.

"Is something wrong, sir? I was told to bring these flowers to the patient in room 412."

The agent gave her a long appraising look.

"This is room 410."

She picked up the flowers, shaking her head, as if in amazement at her mistake.

"I'm so sorry. Let me just get these flowers and I'll get out of the way."

Jacquelyn tightened her grip on the vase as she walked out the door. She felt an itch on her back, as if there were a target there. Any minute she expected an officer to call our for her to halt. She didn't release her breath until she made it out of the room and all the way to the opposite end of the long hallway.

When Jacquelyn glanced toward the room she had just left, she could see a cluster of police and FBI agents standing and conversing in low tones. Now and then an officer would look down the hall at her.

This would be a good time to leave the hospital. Jacquelyn left the flowers at the nurse's station and slid down a hallway, then another.

Jacquelyn escaped to the street outside the hospital. Ducking around the corner to an alley, she pulled off the blond wig and the fake eyelashes and ditched them in a nearby dumpster. Then she took a roundabout way to her car, which she had parked two blocks over.

She slapped the steering wheel, her anger boiling over. Everything was going wrong! The trap in the hospital. Colin Taylor stealing from her. His girlfriend, Rachel, giving the pendant to the police. What kind of woman gave away a valuable piece of jewelry anyway? Brock's stupid move in attacking Colin. The flash drive being gone. What happened to the flash drive? The information on that thumb drive would have netted her a couple million easily.

She thought about who had been waiting in the hospital room. FBI agents. Hmm, someone else found the drive and what was on it. Her entire empire had crashed because of a thief and his girlfriend. She would have to run. Jacquelyn had money stashed in an offshore account for just such an emergency. Still, it made her incredibly angry to have her careful plans completely upset.

Jacquelyn bit her lip as she planned. She would run, but first she would get even with the people who had brought her empire down. She knew she couldn't get to Colin. From what Brock had told her though, Colin would probably be brain damaged anyway. But she would kill Rachel for her part in this fiasco as well.

Brock approached the abandoned deer camp slowly. This time of year, there shouldn't be anyone there. He had a story if he ran into anyone in the woods, but he hoped he wouldn't need it.

As he reached for the door to the cabin, it was yanked open and he found himself face-to-face with his boss. Her expression was one of deep, seething anger. He stepped back in the face of her rage, but Jacquelyn reached out and grabbed a fistful of his shirt, as well as some skin, pulling him into the cabin.

When she released him, Brock moved away from her, his hand going to his chest to rub where she had grabbed him. Though he knew they were supposed to meet, Brock felt dismay at finding her in the hunting cabin.

"Ms. Marquette, what are you doing here? How did you find my hiding place?"

Jacquelyn snorted a very unladylike laugh.

"You're not smart enough to hide from me."

Brock felt the anger begin to boil inside. Jacquelyn loved to use cutting words, but she had not used them on him until the past year. Since then he had seen a change in her demeanor, especially after the loss of the pendant. His boss had become increasingly abusive, both verbally and physically. She even blamed Brock for not catching Colin in the act of stealing from her.

"I wasn't trying to hide from you," he retorted. "I was trying to stay away from the local police. Why would I hide from you? We were actually supposed to be meeting so I could give you an update on the girl."

Jacquelyn tapped her foot impatiently.

"Well, then, give me the update."

Brock took a deep breath, then told Jacquelyn about Rachel's schedule and habits.

"She likes to go out to the stables first thing after breakfast. I guess she likes horses. Seems to like all kinds of animals. Even has a dog that works with the cowboys."

"Does the dog stay with her during the day?"

Jacquelyn didn't like dogs. Brock had even seen her kick at dogs that got too close to her.

"No, the dog is a working animal. Like I just told you, the dog works with the cowboys during the day. At night it stays with the girl."

"Did you search her cabin for the flash drive?"

"Yeah, I did that today. She doesn't have it."

"Are you sure? Did you conduct a thorough search?"

Brock stiffened. He hated when she implied that he didn't know how to do his job.

"Yes, I'm sure. I know how to search, Jacquelyn. I looked all over that cabin. When I left, her things were *almost* the way she had left them."

That was Brock's way of keeping his victim off-balance. He hadn't trashed the cabin, but he had left things a little different. Usually Jacquelyn enjoyed hearing about him toying with people, but today she didn't seem to like anything he said or did.

Brock watched as his employer paced in a tight circle. He could tell she was enraged about something, but knew she would not tell him if he asked. He suspected that her attempt to finish the job on Colin Taylor had not gone well. If it had, Jacquelyn would have come back with a victorious grin and in a celebratory mood. Instead, she was curt and impatient. Her expression was grim and vicious.

"You're fired."

He started out of his reverie.

"What?!"

Jacquelyn glared at him.

"I said you're fired. If you had done your job right, my pendant would not have been stolen. If you had not attacked Colin Taylor in broad daylight, we would not have to be hiding in this flea-infested hovel. You are a stupid, incompetent fool. Everything I worked for has come crashing down and it's your fault!"

Brock felt something hot rise up inside him.

"You know what? I'm glad you fired me. I'm sick of working for you. You're not a woman. You're a cold, heartless monster who uses people and throws them away. You can take your job and . . ."

He stopped when Jacquelyn pulled out her little pistol and pointed it at him. Strangely enough, he wasn't afraid.

"Go ahead," he told her. "Shoot me. I don't care. You have humiliated me for the last time."

With that he turned around and stomped out of the small hunting cabin as the door banged shut behind him.

Jacquelyn slowly lowered the gun. She drew in a deep breath as she realized she shouldn't have fired Brock. Jacquelyn jerked the door open and hurried out.

"Brock!"

He didn't turn or look back. Jacquelyn could see from the rigid way he held himself that her right-hand man was angry. Good. She would use that anger to accomplish her purposes.

"Brock! Come back. I need to talk to you."

Brock stopped and turned to face her.

"I think you said enough."

Jacquelyn caught up to him and reached out to touch his arm. He jerked away and gave her a hostile glare.

"Look, we're both mad right now. I should not have fired you."

"Well, you did, and it's probably best. I don't want to work for you anymore."

"What if I double your pay?"

Brock snorted.

"Yeah, right. Why would you do that? You think I'm stupid and incompetent."

Jacquelyn shook her head.

"That was my anger talking. Look, we've worked well together for the past ten years. You're my right-hand man. I need your special skill set. At least stay with me until I finish my business in this hick town. I want to get even with that fool girl that gave my pendant and flash drive to the police. Then we can both leave this country and start over. I'll help you get a new identity and give you enough money to make your own way."

The big man didn't say anything. He just stared at Jacquelyn until she fidgeted.

"Well? Do we have a deal?"

Brock studied her. The money and new identity sounded good, but he didn't trust Jacquelyn. Finally, he turned and began to walk away. He barely turned his head to answer.

"I'll think about it."

Chapter Eighteen

Jesse was restless. After dinner he played checkers with Spence. He lost both games quickly. Spence started to rib him about it, but stopped and gave him a perceptive look.

"Young man, you have something on your mind?"

Jesse gave him a half-hearted smile.

"I guess I'm just tired. I'm going to head over to the bunkhouse and get some sleep."

Spence nodded.

"Might want to take some time for prayer while you're at it. Seems like the Father might be dealing with you right now."

He was right of course. Jesse had felt God's tug on him all day. Actually, for several days. He had tried to stay busy because he wasn't sure he could face why God was convicting him.

Jesse waved another cowhand to his seat in front of the checkers board and headed for the door. He wandered down the path past the cabins. He saw Rachel's cabin sitting dark and quiet and felt a moment of thankfulness that Kendall had insisted that Rachel and Angel stay in the main house until Maggie could catch whoever had broken into the cabin.

He stopped at the paddock and leaned against the

fence, his eyes taking in the panorama of stars in the summer sky. He could feel a gentle breeze brushing his face. The sounds of animals settling in for the night were soothing to him. Jesse loved working at the ranch. Kendall had already told him that he could stay even after his five years of probation were up. Maybe one day he could have his own ranch.

Jesse sighed as he looked at the sky again. It seemed everyone knew what was wrong with him. Lately he had read and reread 1 John 1:9, trying to wrap his mind around the idea that God could cleanse him. He felt convicted about holding on to his past. Tears stung his eyes as Jesse felt the urge to pray.

"God," he began. "You know my past. Several people have told me that since I accepted Christ as my Savior and Lord, all my past has been forgiven and wiped clean."

He turned toward the fence around the paddock and hit a post with his fist.

"But, Lord, it hurts every time I think about those kids I sold drugs to. How many of them became addicted? How many overdosed?"

Jesse was crying now.

"Lord, I can't stand it anymore. Please take this burden of fear and guilt from me. I can't carry it. It's too heavy. If You've forgiven me, then I know I need to forgive myself. But I can't do it alone. The memories keep coming back. And there are people in this town who won't let me forget."

The tears slid down his cheeks as Jesse knelt in silence for a long time. He seemed to hear God's voice reminding him that His Son died for all the sins of the world, including Jesse's. Those sins were nailed to the cross. Christ's resurrection removed their power. Hope began to bubble up inside Jesse.

He stood and wiped the tears from his face.

"Thank You, Father," he breathed. "Thank You for Your awesome gifts of mercy and grace. Just as You've forgiven me, I choose to forgive myself and others."

Jesse felt lighter and freer than he had ever felt. He couldn't wait to tell Rachel what had happened. He glanced at the windows in the main house and saw that the light in her room was off. Tomorrow, he decided. He would tell her tomorrow. And he would ask if she was still interested in seeing where their relationship could go. He still felt that he didn't deserve her. But he didn't deserve God's grace either, and God had given him that.

His smile came from somewhere deep inside as he headed into the bunkhouse. Jesse whistled a hymn as he readied for bed. For the first time in a long time, he slept deeply and restfully, his heavy burden gone.

"Okay, guys, let's get moving," Kendall urged. "We have a lot of chores that need doing today."

Jason shoveled in a huge bite of scrambled eggs and hash browns as he reached for another of Rachel's delicious cinnamon rolls. Jesse caught Rachel's eye and smiled at the scene. It was like this at every meal. Jason ate as if he would never get to eat again. Rachel grinned back at Jesse. She loved to see people enjoying the food she prepared.

Jesse hurried to carry his plate to the sink and stopped to talk to Rachel.

"Can you meet me out at the main stable after you finish the breakfast dishes? I have something important to tell you."

"You could just tell me here while you help with the dishes," she teased.

Rachel could see there was something different about Jesse. She couldn't wait to talk to him and find out what was going on.

"No thanks." He recoiled in mock horror.

"Dishes are my least favorite chore. Besides, Kendall wants me to check around the stables for holes and loose boards. We've had some small animals sneaking into the stable and getting into the feed for the cattle and horses."

"You could get Angel to help you. She's good at finding holes."

Jesse had to laugh at that. Angel did seem to have a knack for finding holes in the barn and stables. Cowhands often found her waiting for them in the locked barn.

Rachel nodded.

"It won't take me long to get these loaded in the dishwasher and get everything wiped down. I'll be out in about fifteen or twenty minutes."

Jesse headed for the back door.

"I'll give you twenty in case Jason keeps eating."

Kendall came back into the kitchen.

"Jason! It's time to stop eating and get to work. Let's go, cowboy!"

Jason took one more gulp of his juice, then stood and brushed crumbs off of his shirt onto the floor. Rachel rolled her eyes at the extra work he was making for her, but didn't say anything. She and Jason had made their peace, but he still had a very defensive attitude and she didn't want to start the morning with an argument.

Jesse called her name just before he left.

"Don't forget, okay, Rachel? I have something really important to tell you."

She smiled back at him.

"I'll be there."

Maggie set her phone down slowly, a thoughtful look on her face. One of her son's friends had told his parents about seeing a strange woman camping out in the woods where the boys liked to hike. Maggie told the parent to tell their son to hold off on any hiking in those woods until she could check it out. She picked up her phone and dialed Robert's number.

"Hello?"

"Hi son, it's Mom."

"Hi, Mom. What's up? Do you have something you want me to do today?"

Robert had been so excited and grateful to get not just a flash drive for his music, but an MP3 player and headphones, that he had been offering to do extra chores for Maggie. She had to smile at his eagerness. He was a good kid.

"No son, no extra chores today. Listen, your buddy, Mike, saw a strange woman in the woods where you two like to go hiking. I want you to stay out of the woods until I can check it out. Something doesn't seem right about that."

"Aw, Mom! That's our favorite place to go!"

"I know, but for your safety I want you two to stay out of there. Go swimming or stay at the house and play some games."

There was silence on the phone for a moment. Finally, Robert spoke again.

"Well, it is kind of creepy to think about that strange lady in our woods. Okay, we can hang out here. Mike said he wants another chance to beat me at Monopoly."

"That's a great idea. You can even pop some popcorn in the microwave."

"Can we have some soda?"

"You may have one can each."

"Only one? That popcorn can be kind of salty."

Maggie tried not to smile at his wheedling tone. Failing that, she worked to inject a stern note into her voice.

"One soda or none."

After getting his solemn promise that he would limit the soda and junk food while his friend was visiting, Maggie hung up and dialed Monica.

"Hey, Maggie, I was just about to call you. I have some information about Jacquelyn Marquette, alias about a dozen other names. She's got her fingers on a number of shady operations. She's also got a prison record. "

Maggie's face grew grim as Monica filled her in on Jacquelyn. She told Monica about the report of a strange woman seen in the woods that the boys hiked in.

"I told Robert to stay out of the woods."

"Good idea," Monica told her. Then she paused as if she wanted to say something.

"What are you thinking?"

"You know, we found that necklace in her hotel room in Shreveport, but the tracker was gone. I wonder why this woman is hanging around your little town. She already knows the flash drive is gone and she can't get to Colin Taylor. What else would she want?"

Both women thought in silence for a moment, then it hit them.

"Rachel! She's after Rachel James. She probably blames Rachel for that flash drive going missing since Rachel turned the necklace in to me."

"Maggie, I have a warrant for her arrest for industrial espionage. I'll round up some agents and meet you at that ranch. What's its name?"

"The Rocking K. I'll meet you there. We need to get to Rachel before Jacquelyn Marquette does."

Chapter Nineteen

"Give me a few minutes and I'll help with the calves," Jesse shouted to the cowboys. He could see them mounting up and heading to a pasture on the far side of the ranch. He turned to the stable in time to see Rachel going through the door looking for him.

"Hey."

Jesse spoke softly as he entered so he wouldn't startle her. Rachel turned at the sound of his voice.

"Hey yourself."

Rachel studied Jesse.

"You look different somehow. You seem more at peace."

"That's what I wanted to talk to you about. Something happened last night. Something that changed me."

Rachel listened as Jesse shared what he experienced the night before. When he got to the part about giving God his burden of guilt and fear, her eyes glistened with unshed tears. By the time he finished telling her all of it, both of them had tears running down their faces.

"Jesse, I'm so glad for you. I know you've been carrying a heavy burden for a while, but you wouldn't talk about it."

"That's because I felt like I deserved to feel guilty. Now I realize it was wrong for me to hold on to that guilt. Like the song says, Jesus paid it all."

He laid his hands on Rachel's shoulders, meeting her tearful gaze with his.

"Rachel, when I kissed you, I pulled away because I felt that I didn't deserve you because of my past. But, now, well."

He hesitated.

"Jesse, like you said, Jesus forgave you. If our great God can forgive, certainly I can't hold anything against you."

She gave him an impish grin.

"Not even when you give me a hard time about my truck."

Jesse returned her grin with one of his own.

"Well, that truck is a whole 'nother story."

He sobered again.

"Rachel, I do have feelings for you. The fact is, I've fallen in love with you. I would like to see where our relationship could go, if you're still willing."

Rachel took one of his hands from her shoulder and held it against her cheek.

"I'm still willing."

Jesse pulled her close and tenderly kissed her. She wound her arms around his neck and deepened the kiss. After the kiss ended, Jesse leaned his forehead against Rachel's, his expression one of awe.

"Wow! God is good!"

"All the time," she responded, running her hand down his jaw.

They stood holding each other for a few minutes, then Jesse reluctantly stepped back.

"I wish I could stay here with you, but I promised I'd help round up some calves today."

"I know. But we'll see each other tonight."

Jesse gave her a quick kiss, then turned to leave. At the door he looked back with a huge smile.

"I love you Rachel James. I want to tell the whole world."

"I love you too, Jesse Williams. I just might go tell the whole world."

They were both laughing as he walked out the door.

Jesse mounted his gelding and rode toward the other hands to help with rounding up the calves. The cowboys saw the expression on his face and the teasing began.

"Hey, look y'all! I think Jesse's in love."

"I don't think it. I know it. Who is it Jess? Is it our pretty little cook?"

"Hey, that's no fair! I had my eye on her."

One of the other guys snorted.

"You? You're much too ugly for her."

"Who you callin' ugly? You looked in the mirror lately?"

Jesse just shook his head as he grinned at them. He knew the guys were actually glad for him. The more they teased, the more they showed their support.

"So, lover boy, when's the wedding?"

He stopped to think about it.

"I still have to ask her to marry me," he finally admitted.

"What's taking you so long?" they shouted. "Get to it, boy!"

While the men were joking and working the calves, Angel was busy doing her job herding the calves. The cowboys were surprised when the little dog stopped and turned her attention away from the cattle. Her ears swiveled and her head snapped around to stare at the building housing the horses. She ran part way toward the stables, then turned to look at the cowhands. Her stare said she needed them to come with her.

"Hey, Angel! Come back here! Heel, girl!"

As the Border Collie ran circles around them and barked, trying to move the cowboys back toward the ranch house and stables, Spence raised his hand.

"Hey! You fellas listen to me! I think Angel's on to something. She's a right smart dog. Maybe something bad is happening at the stables and she's trying to get our attention and tell us about it."

Jesse remembered when he first met Rachel and Angel; how the little dog had herded him toward Rachel's broken-down truck. He wheeled his horse around to gallop back, shouting over his shoulder:

"Rachel's in trouble. Come on, let's go!"

The other hands looked at Spence who nodded grimly.

"You heard the man. Let's go!"

The cowhands arrived at the stable about the same time several Forrestville squad cars and a half dozen dark blue sedans pulled into the driveway. They found Jesse outside the barn, trying to get in. He pulled on the big doors but couldn't budge them.

Maggie led the officers and FBI agents to the group clustered around the stable doors.

"What's going on?"

Jesse shook the doors in frustration.

"We think Rachel's in trouble in there, but the door is barred and we can't get in!"

Fear and frustration trembled in his voice.

Maggie sent her officers to check around the building for a way to get in. A few of the cowboys went with them to help.

Jesse noticed Angel sniffing around and remembered the holes that he had not filled yet. Just then the little dog disappeared through a hole into the stable.

"Hey guys, I think Angel's found a way in."

Jesse watched her tail vanish into a dark hole.

"I hope she can help," he muttered. "God, please protect Rachel, and Angel too!"

Rachel wandered down the length of the stables, stopping to pet the horses that had not been taken to round up the calves. She was so happy she was humming as she went. Jesse loved her! It was all so wonderful. She could hardly believe it.

At least it would be if not for the strange uneasy feeling in the pit of her stomach. Something wasn't right. Rachel had a strange feeling that someone was watching her. She wanted to ignore it and enjoy what was the best day ever. But she knew better than to ignore her instincts. Rachel stopped and listened.

She heard a sound behind her like a piece of wood sliding, and turned to see a stranger barring the stable door. When Rachel looked closer, she saw an older woman, still beautiful, but with a grim, determined smile on her face. She realized this was the woman Colin had been so afraid of; the woman Maggie had told them about - Jacquelyn Marquette.

"It didn't take you long to get a new boyfriend, did it?" Jacquelyn sneered.

Rachel stood quietly, warily watching the woman. She forced herself to slow her breathing and relax her muscles. She knew being tense and anxious would make it difficult for her to defend herself and maintain control.

"I can see why Colin would come on to you," Jacquelyn continued. "You are a pretty little thing. Probably have all these cowboys hanging all over you."

Jacquelyn moved closer to Rachel.

"But I didn't come here to talk about your love life. I came here to kill you."

Rachel's eyes widened, but she still did not answer.

"That's right. You and Colin have been nothing but trouble for me. Colin never should have taken what was mine and given it to you."

Rachel finally answered her.

"Colin did not give me that necklace. He hid it in my suitcase. When I left in a hurry, I didn't notice it until recently. Since it is not mine, I gave it to the police."

"Yes! You gave it to the police and they found the flash drive with information that would have earned me millions of dollars. Now my whole business is ruined and I have to go somewhere and start over. It's all your fault!"

Rachel realized that Jacquelyn was in an irrational and dangerous state of mind. She looked around for a way out. Jacquelyn laughed at her.

"I barred the door. All the cowboys are gone chasing cows, as is your dog. No one will come to your rescue, young lady."

She walked to within a few feet of Rachel and laughed again, the sound sending chills down Rachel's spine. The laugh sounded almost hysterical. She knew this woman was out of control.

"I saw what you did to my employee."

At Rachel's look of surprise, Jacquelyn nodded, clearly enjoying having the upper hand.

"Yes, Brock works for me. I almost fired him for being stupid. He never should have attacked you and Colin in public. But I must say, I admire your self-defense moves."

She moved to strike Rachel. When Rachel blocked her, Jacquelyn jabbed her in the ribs with the other hand. Rachel gasped in pain as Jacquelyn stepped back and studied her.

"You see, Rachel James, you're not the only one who knows self-defense. Just between us girls, I was in prison for a short time. I learned a few things while I was there, like how to fight dirty. And I don't mind fighting dirty."

With that she launched herself at Rachel, her hands and feet a blur as she kicked and punched the frightened young woman over and over. Rachel was able to block some, but many blows found their mark. Finally, Rachel landed a blow that knocked the older woman back a few feet at the same time that Jacquelyn kicked her in the shoulder, causing Rachel to stumble back.

Rachel stood trying to catch her breath and feeling the pain in her shoulder. She could feel the panic that preceded loss of control try to take hold. This crazy woman was strong, capable, and out to kill her! What could she do? How could she defend herself? She ached all over and her strength was draining away. Fear began to bubble up inside.

She threw herself at Jacquelyn in blind rage, kicking and striking wildly. Jacquelyn laughed and easily blocked the blows, returning them with punches that ignited the pain in Rachel's shoulder. Finally, she struck Rachel across the face, causing her to fall backward. Rachel lay stunned for a moment, trying to breathe through the pain in her body. She managed to get to her knees, but could not rise to her feet.

"Help me, God!"

Rachel turned to her new Friend.

"I'm scared. I need Your help!"

She felt a calmness come over her as she recalled her Uncle Jon's voice.

Rachel, you have the techniques down, but you have no control. You just react in fear and panic. That will either get you killed or get your opponent killed. You need to think before you move. You need to keep control of yourself so you can take control of your opponent. Remember, to knowledge add self-control."

She looked up to see Jacquelyn watching her with a triumphant smirk on her face.

"What's wrong?" she sneered. "Can't handle a real fighter? Go ahead, catch your breath. I think I will rather enjoy a good fight before I kill you."

Rachel just got to her feet and stood quietly, allowing God's peace to fill her and give her strength.

Before Jacquelyn could move again, they heard a sound like something digging. Suddenly a black and white blur shot across the room.

It was Angel! She had dug through one of the holes that Jesse was supposed to fill in. Now she was barking and snarling at Jacquelyn. The older woman stood with a look of fear and hatred marring her lovely face. Then her foot snapped out, catching the Border Collie in the middle and throwing her several feet away.

Angel's yelp of pain galvanized Rachel. That evil woman had hurt her dog! The rage Rachel felt threatened to engulf her and undo the peace she had just experienced. She wanted to tear Jacquelyn to pieces. Then, as if a cool hand was laid on her forehead, Rachel heard Esther's words from their training.

"Take the anger and fear and use it, Rachel. Don't let it control you. Let it help you focus on your objective, which is to defeat your opponent with the least amount of harm to the both of you."

Rachel watched as Jacquelyn's expression changed from one of triumph to one of puzzlement. She took in long slow breaths and drew on her training. Rachel lifted a desperate prayer.

"God, please help me defeat this evil woman without losing control of myself."

Then she began a controlled assault on Jacquelyn, striking and kicking with precision. Jacquelyn managed a few strikes and kicks, but they had no effect. Finally, Rachel struck Jacquelyn with a strong blow, knocking her across the dirt floor.

Rachel stood, watching her opponent. It seemed that Jacquelyn was out, for now. The woman lay motionless on the stable floor. As Rachel began to relax, she saw a large form emerge from the shadows. It was the man who had attacked Colin! Rachel's heart rate jumped. What was he doing here? How long had he been in the stables? Was she going to have to fight him now?

He moved to stand beside Jacquelyn's still form, but did not reach to help her. He just stood staring at her, his expression unreadable. Jacquelyn's eyes opened and a triumphant grin spread across her face. She struggled to a sitting position.

"Brock! I am glad to see you."

She pointed at Rachel.

"Get that woman! She's the one responsible for all our problems."

At first Brock did not move. Then he reached out a meaty hand and grabbed Jacquelyn by the front of her jacket, lifting her high in the air and holding her where her feet could not touch the floor.

"No, Jacquelyn. YOU are the reason for all our problems. But I will take care of that right now."

With that he threw her several feet away. She hit the ground hard and lay still. At first, Rachel thought the older woman might be dead. Then she heard a groan escape from her.

Angel rose and staggered over to stand in front of Rachel, growls rumbling from her throat.

Brock turned to look at them and shook his head.

"It's okay, lady. I'm done doing her dirty work. Tell your dog it's okay. I won't hurt you."

Rachel was doubtful about calling off Angel. Suddenly the dog darted toward Jacquelyn. The woman was trying to sit up, but the Collie stood over her, snarling and staring into her eyes. Jacquelyn fell back to the floor with another groan.

Rachel heard voices outside the door. The cowboys were trying to break through the door. She could hear Jesse's frantic voice calling for her.

She backed toward the door and slid the bar back, keeping a watchful glance on Brock and Jacquelyn. Jesse swooped in and enfolded her in his arms.

"Are you okay?"

Rachel nodded.

"I am now."

FBI agents and local police swarmed into the stable, guns drawn. They eyed Brock standing near Jacquelyn, who was still on the ground. Maggie patted Angel on the head and told her what a good girl she was. Then she caught Rachel's eye and nodded toward the dog.

"Angel, heel!"

The little dog trotted over to sit beside Rachel.

Maggie flipped Jacquelyn over and snapped handcuffs on her, then hauled her to her feet, ignoring the woman's groans and complaints.

"Jacquelyn Marquette, you're under arrest!"

As the officers led Jacquelyn and Brock away, the big man was already offering to provide testimony; even while Jacquelyn hurled invectives at him, threatening to kill him.

Jesse took Rachel in his arms again. Both of them were trembling from fear and relief that it was over.

"I was so scared something would happen to you," he told her.

"I was kind of scared myself," she confessed. "But when she kicked Angel, I felt something come over me. I was enraged at her for kicking my dog, but God helped me to stay in control."

Jesse tightened his hold on her, grateful for God protecting Rachel again.

Chapter Twenty

"Rachel, are you sure you're okay?"

Kendall and the ranch's hands hovered over Rachel. They would not allow her to cook or clean that evening, so dinner was an interesting meal.

They had decided on sandwiches, but then couldn't find half the ingredients they needed. Rachel wanted to just jump up and run into the kitchen, but she was held in place by Jesse on one side and Spence on the other.

"Hold on, young lady," the old cowboy smiled. "They can get by for one evening. You just rest."

Jesse squeezed her shoulder. He hadn't let her out of his sight since he found her in the stables.

"He's right, hon."

He laughed.

"I bet they end up ordering pizza, though."

"Just shows what you know, hot shot."

Kendall picked up the phone. She was grinning as she dialed, then answered him while waiting for the phone to ring.

"We're ordering barbecue."

The three on the couch laughed, although for Rachel the threat of tears lingered underneath. The outpouring of love from her boss and the hands touched Rachel deeply.

Most of all seeing the light of love in Jesse's eyes sent a thrill through her. She wondered about the look she had seen in his eyes all afternoon. It was as if he was up to something.

Later, after dinner, Jesse walked her to her cabin. He checked the door to make sure it was locked, then made her stand just inside the door. He called Angel to guard her while he checked every corner of the tiny cabin.

Finally, satisfied that everything was safe, Jesse pulled Rachel into his arms and kissed her soundly. He held her and sighed.

"Rachel, when I saw you in the stable with that woman and that big evil-looking man, I thought my heart would stop.

Jesse paused and swallowed hard.

"I couldn't help thinking that we just found out how much we love each other and I could have lost you."

"I know, Jesse. I was thinking the same thing. When she told me she was going to kill me, I was thinking that we wouldn't get to see where things would go in our relationship."

Jesse pulled away from her.

"I know where I want things to go," he said. Then he dropped to one knee and pulled something out of his pocket.

"Rachel, I feel like you are a precious gift that God has given to me. Completely undeserved; a gift from His grace. If you feel it's too soon, I'll understand. But, I do love you. Will you marry me?"

Rachel gazed down at him for so long, Jesse was afraid she would say no. Then he saw the happy tears in her eyes and the big smile on her face.

"Yes!" she almost shouted. "No, it's not too soon. Yes, I will marry you."

Jesse slid a ring on her hand. It was a thin band of gold with a small pearl surrounded by small diamonds.

"This was my mother's engagement ring," he said softly. "Aunt Abigail gave it to me a few years ago and told me to never put it on any woman's hand until I was sure she was the one God has for me. I've never been more sure of anything in my life. *You* are the one for me."

The tears spilled from Rachel's eyes down her cheeks. Jesse stood and wiped her tears with his thumbs.

"Are those happy tears?"

She smiled back at him.

"You bet they are."

They stood in each other's arms for a few moments, then Jesse sighed.

"What's wrong?"

Rachel studied his face, seeing the beginning of worry.

"Maybe I shouldn't have asked you so soon. Rachel, I'm still on probation. When my five years is up in a couple of years, I can still work at the Rocking K, but how will I provide for you and our children?"

"Whoa, cowboy! One thing at a time. We don't have those children yet. I can continue to work here too. Maybe Kendall would let us use this cabin for a while until we can work out something else. Let's ask God to handle the details for us, okay?"

Jesse squeezed her.

"I love seeing how you've grown in your faith, Rachel. You're right, I need to stop worrying and trust God to handle the details. You want to pray with me about it?"

"I can't think of a better way to start our lives together as a couple."

Chapter Twenty-One

Jesse and Rachel stepped inside the diner and paused to search for their friends. Rachel saw David and Christy first, then Esther and Stephen. She waved to them and pulled Jesse toward their table.

"Sweetie, are you okay?"

Rachel hugged Christy, then stepped back so the older woman could search her eyes. Christy must have been satisfied at what she saw, because she squeezed Rachel again before letting her go.

"That was quite an ordeal you went through, young lady."

David's eyes were concerned as he glanced at Rachel. His wife nudged him and nodded toward the ring on Rachel's hand.

"It looks like things have worked out for you two," she added. "Congratulations!"

Rachel blushed, then turned to answer David, her gaze including Stephen and Esther who sat forward to listen to her.

"It was very scary for me," Rachel admitted. "Jacquelyn Marquette is a cold, hard woman who told me she doesn't mind fighting dirty. She almost had me at one point. I was ready to give up when Angel somehow got into the stable and came to my defense. When Jacquelyn kicked my dog, that somehow spurred me into action."

Here she turned to her instructor, her face glowing with excitement.

"I almost lost control and that woman almost defeated me. When she knocked me down, I prayed and asked God to help me. After Jacquelyn Marquette hurt Angel, I wanted to tear her in pieces, but I didn't lose control, Esther. God helped me to keep my cool and use the training from my dad, my uncle, and you. I think I need to thank you for giving me the tools I needed to defend myself without losing control."

Esther gave her a sweet smile of approval.

"No, Rachel. Give God the glory for that. He's the one who helped you use all the tools of your lifetime."

The others chimed in their agreement. Rachel blinked back tears.

"You're right. I need to thank God for helping me in that awful situation."

She allowed a sly grin to come through.

"I'll also thank Him for giving you to me as my instructor."

The waitress came up just then, handed them menus and took their drink orders. Then she left to serve another table.

Jesse looked up and saw Maggie standing in the doorway. He put his hand on Rachel's arm and nodded toward the police chief.

"How about if we invite Maggie to join us?"

"Sounds good to me. Are the rest of you okay with that?"

They all voiced their agreement and waved Maggie to their table.

"I'm glad I caught you while you're in town," she told them. "Saves me a trip out to the ranch."

"What's up?"

Rachel wondered if something else had happened. She squeezed Jesse's hand under the table, seeking reassurance. He squeezed back, then slid his arm around her shoulders.

Maggie glanced at the other two couples then back at Jesse and Rachel with a question in her eyes.

"I think I'd like them to know what's going on too," Rachel said. Maggie nodded as she sat and pulled her chair closer.

"Jacquelyn is in federal custody. My contact in the FBI tells me they have enough on her to put her away for a long time. Especially since her, uh, employee, Brock, is telling them everything he knows. Brock will go to prison too. Both of them have federal and state charges against them."

Maggie turned to Rachel.

"I hear you did some impressive fighting in there. It takes a lot to impress a man like Brock, but he was definitely impressed."

"Was she injured?" Rachel wanted to know. "I don't think I hurt anything except her pride. But she was thrown pretty hard by that man, and he's big and powerful!"

Maggie shook her head.

"She had a few cracked ribs and a mild concussion. I think she got off pretty easy. You're right. Brock is a big man and could have easily killed her. Apparently she's been abusing and humiliating him for a long time. He got his fill of it. But you don't have to worry about either one of them anymore."

"You also don't have to worry about Colin Taylor ever bothering you again. He sustained a pretty substantial head injury when Brock rammed him into that brick wall.

In light of his injuries, he will probably not have to serve any time for theft. Besides, if he had not stolen that necklace, we never would have found the stolen information on the flash drive inside."

Rachel sat still for a moment; a sad, thoughtful expression on her face. Jesse slid his arm around her shoulder.

"What are you thinking, sweetheart?"

Rachel looked up at him.

"I think I feel sad for him. I know what he did was wrong - stealing and trying to assault me. But he will live in a different kind of prison for the rest of his life."

The mood at the table was somber for a moment, then Maggie injected a bright note.

"Hey, I hear congratulations are in order. When is the big day?"

Rachel and Jesse looked at each other and smiled. Then they turned to the others.

"We don't know yet," they chorused. Then Jesse flashed a grin.

"But it will be soon," he asserted. "Very soon."

Rachel elbowed him as they all laughed.

"You've got your hands full, there, Rachel," Maggie warned her. Then the police chief turned to Jesse.

"Because of yours and Rachel's help with this case, I might be able to get the judge to take some time off of your probation. Let me check on that and I'll let you know."

Chapter Twenty-Two

It was a beautiful September day when Jesse and Rachel drove to Marcus Taylor's home in Austin, Texas to let Rachel talk with her former employer. The air was cool and surprisingly dry for that part of the country. They had driven in the day before and stayed in separate rooms at a local motel. Now they were headed to the Taylor estate.

Rachel's stomach cramped as they turned down the street toward the place that was her home for several years. She knew she was doing the right thing, coming back to tell Mr. Taylor why she ran, but it was still very hard to do.

She was going to have to tell the man who had been nothing but kind to her that his nephew, probably his heir, had tried to rape her and that she had nearly killed him. Then she had run instead of coming to her boss and explaining everything to him. Rachel wouldn't blame him if he never wanted anything to do with her again.

Jesse reached across the seat and took her hand, threading his fingers through hers.

"You don't have to do this, you know."

Rachel looked down, fighting the tears.

"Yes, I do. It's the right thing to do. It's just really hard."

Jesse squeezed her hand, then lifted it to his lips.

"I'll be right there with you."

Rachel gave him a tremulous smile.

"I know. Thank you for coming with me."

They pulled through the gate and around the circular drive. As Jesse helped Rachel out of his truck, they saw the front door to the main house open and Marcus Taylor step out. His face lit up when he saw her. He hurried toward the couple and enfolded her in a hug.

"Rachel! I am so glad to see you! Are you all right? I've been incredibly worried about you."

Rachel swiped tears from her cheeks as she introduced Jesse to Marcus. The older man shook Jesse's hand warmly.

"You be good to this young lady, now. She's very special to me."

Rachel fidgeted a bit.

"Mr. Taylor, I have something I need to tell you. Can we go in the house and talk for a few minutes?"

"Sure! Where are my manners? Come on in and have something to drink."

They entered the front hall. Rachel looked around and noticed a few changes. Marcus saw her looking around and laughed.

"My new housekeeper has been redecorating my space. It seems she has aspirations toward becoming an interior decorator and she's practicing on me."

Rachel gave a small chuckle. After they were seated she began.

"Mr. Taylor, I need to apologize for leaving the way I did. I came back to explain. After I tell you my story, I will understand if you never want anything else to do with me."

Marcus looked puzzled.

"Rachel, I can't imagine you doing anything that would have that effect on me. I was worried about you when you disappeared. But, I'm not angry with you."

Jesse squeezed Rachel's hand and nodded encouragingly at her. She took a deep breath and began. She told the whole story - the attempted rape, her choking Colin, thinking he was dead and running out of fear that no one would believe her about the assault. She also told about the necklace and what had happened over the past few months in Forrestville and at the Rocking K.

Her former employer listened intently, an unreadable expression on his face. When she finished, he sat in silence for a few minutes. Rachel could feel her heart pounding. Would he be angry? Would he demand her arrest for assault on his nephew? Then his words caught her by surprise.

"Oh, Rachel, I am so sorry you had to go through all that. I feel it is partly my fault. I knew Colin was flirting with you and could see that you were not comfortable around him. I should have said something to him. I should have told him to leave you alone. As for the stealing, I had no idea that Colin was doing that. I can't say that I'm surprised, though. He was always a thrill seeker. Stealing and getting away with it would give him that adrenaline rush he wanted."

"I . . .I'm sorry, Uncle Marcus. I know that I d..d..did wrong."

The three of them looked up to see Colin walking slowly into the room. His old cockiness was gone and his once confident stride was now an unsteady gait.

Marcus got up and went to help his nephew to a seat. When he saw Rachel's questioning look, he explained.

"Colin has been in rehab for traumatic brain injury. He's on a weekend visit right now."

Colin raised his hand part way as if asking permission to speak.

"R..Rachel, I'm s.s.sorry."

Her heart twisted hearing the slow, halting words from a man she once feared and despised. She leaned forward encouragingly.

"Mr. Taylor," she began, then looked at Marcus. "Colin, I want you to know that because Christ has forgiven me, I can forgive you. I hope for only the best for you now and I will pray for your healing."

"Th..Thank you. S.s.someone at the r . .rehab center told me about Jesus. I . .I'm th..thinking about what they said."

He sagged a little, then looked at his uncle.

"I think I..I need to go r.rest now."

Marcus rang a bell for the housekeeper who bustled in and helped Colin out of the chair and down the hall to his room.

After they left, Marcus looked toward Rachel.

"I think there's something else I should tell you. I know Colin, and probably you, were under the impression that, because I have no children and Colin is my only nephew, he would be my only heir. But that's not true."

He smiled at Rachel.

"You see, my dear, you were more than a cook and housekeeper to me. When I hired you, you were just a young girl trying to make her way in the world. When your father died and your uncle was severely injured, I was glad I could provide you a place to live as well as a way to earn your living. Rachel, you are a very special young lady to me, almost like my own daughter. Colin is my main heir, but you will inherit one-third of my estate."

Rachel was stunned. She had expected recrimination and blame, not this!

"Oh, no, Mr. Taylor, I can't be your heir. That's too much for the little service I gave. Especially when you consider what I did to Colin."

"I love my nephew, but I have to say - he got what he deserved then. His injury has actually been a blessing because it has caused him to take a good look at his life and work out some changes for the better. I'm just sorry you had to go through such a hard time. I wouldn't blame you if you held me partly responsible. As your employer and friend, I should have protected you better."

Marcus stood and walked over to Rachel. He held out his hand to her. She stood and clasped his hand with both of hers. Then he pulled her into a hug. When the hug ended, both of them had tears in their eyes. Then he looked at her left hand.

"So, you two are engaged? When is the big day?"

Jesse rose and pulled Rachel to his side.

"In one month, at the ranch where we both work - the Rocking K."

Rachel added her voice.

"We would love for you to come. Uncle Jon is going to come too. He's done with his rehab and has come to Forrestville to live. It's a small wedding, just the staff at the ranch and a few friends from town."

Marcus gave them a huge grin.

"I would love to come! I know it's early, but I would like to give you a wedding present now."

Rachel tried to protest, but Marcus waved her off.

"Nonsense! This is from an old family friend. You'll hurt my feelings if you don't accept it."

He left the room to retrieve his gift for them. After he left, Jesse pulled Rachel close.

"I bet you're glad that's over."

She gave him a radiant smile.

"Actually, I don't feel like that. Everything went so much better than I could have ever hoped for."

Marcus came back into the room a few minutes later and handed them a beautifully wrapped box.

"You can open it before the wedding, but not until after you leave Austin. Now, how about an early dinner? I heard my cook say it's just about ready. She has some women's thing to go to tonight, so she prepared early. I must say, I'm starving. How about you?"

Epilogue

Rachel sat with her hand entwined with Jesse's, watching as their ranch family and friends mingled and enjoyed the wedding feast. Rachel was so happy she felt her heart would burst.

The wedding had been incredible. Kendall and a few other hands built an arch for Jesse and Rachel to stand under for saying their vows. They festooned the arch with flowers and greenery. Other hands set up rows of folding chairs and decorated the ends with white bows.

Kendall told them that of course they could continue to work for her.

"Just try to get away," she told them with a telltale glimmer in her eye.

Then she offered them the use of a larger cabin that sat a little further behind the bunkhouse and small cabins the rest of the staff used.

When the day of the wedding arrived, Jesse stayed sequestered in the bunkhouse until almost time for the ceremony. When Rachel saw him as she floated up the aisle on the arm of her Uncle Jon, she thought he was the handsomest man on earth. Jesse wore a navy blue suit with a white dress shirt and light blue tie. His intense brown eyes held her gaze all the way up the aisle.

Rachel felt radiant in her tea-length white dress. Instead of a veil, she chose to wear a crown of white roses in her hair, which she had allowed to grow out and return to its natural dark auburn color. The curled ends brushed her shoulders, accentuating her creamy skin and the pink tint that glowed in her cheeks.

Angel, of course, had to be part of the wedding. The guests laughed as they saw the Border Collie, wearing her wedding collar of flowers, carrying a small basket of rose petals down the aisle ahead of the bride. They couldn't help being impressed as Angel shook the basket slightly, scattering petals as she went.

Marcus Taylor came for the wedding. He looked at Rachel and Jesse with a knowing glint in his eyes. The gift he had given them was a check for $50,000. When Rachel saw that number on the check, her first thought had been to refuse. Jesse reminded her that Marcus said it was a gift from an old family friend.

"You'll really hurt him if you don't accept the gift," he told her.

Because of the gift, the couple was able to plan a honeymoon in the Ozarks. The two of them agreed that the Ozarks in mid-October would be a beautiful place to begin their life together. Jesse and Rachel planned to drive to northern Arkansas and spend a week there, leaving Angel with Kendall. Then they would return to the ranch and to the jobs they loved.

"What are you thinking about?"

Jesse's breath was warm on her neck as he pulled Rachel close.

"Just how wonderfully everything came together for our special day."

Rachel's eyes were shining.

"Jesse, don't you feel all the love that went into making this a day of wonderful memories?"

He smiled tenderly at his bride.

"Yes, I do. And I'm ready to begin our honeymoon of wonderful memories. You ready to go?"

Rachel blushed and nodded.

Jesse stood and pulled her to her feet. Holding her hand tightly in his, he waved the other hand to get their friends' attention.

"It's time for us to get on the road. Thanks everyone for a terrific day!"

Their friends and family gathered around for hugs and well-wishes. Then Jesse helped Rachel into his truck and got in on his side. He turned the key and heard nothing. He tried again with the same result. Shaking his head in disbelief he popped the hood and got out of the truck to check the engine.

Willie trotted over and looked with him. After poking around a bit, the mechanic shook his head and gave Jesse a doleful look.

"Well, Jesse, I hate to tell you this on your weddin' day, but you ain't goin' anywhere in this truck. From the looks of things, it will take me about a week to get the parts and get it fixed. Of course, I'll know more when I get it on my rack."

Jesse groaned, but Rachel gave him a mischievous look.

"That's okay, Willie. You take the truck in and do what you have to do. Jesse, we'll take my truck. It will at least get us to Shreveport. Then we can rent a car for the rest of the trip."

Her new husband looked at her in horror.

"Take the rust bucket?! On our honeymoon?"

Rachel looped her arm through his.

"Just to get to Shreveport," she wheedled. "Come on, we need to get going."

They moved their stuff to Rachel's old truck, got in, and waved goodbye again. Jesse turned the key and sagged with relief when the engine started.

They drove down the long driveway and turned onto the highway. Before the ranch was out of sight, the old truck began shuddering and slowing as smoke began to pour from under the hood.

Rachel laughed.

"I think this is where I came in."

Dear Reader,

Thank you for reading *Hidden Target.* Jesse and Rachel each had a long, difficult road to finding and accepting God's forgiveness.

Rachel flees after using extreme means to defend herself. She fears going to jail, but she's mostly afraid she will lose control and hurt someone else. She believes there is no way God can forgive her for killing a man. Jesse knows God has forgiven him, but he can't forgive himself for selling drugs to children. He tries to earn the mercy and grace extended to him.

The beginning of their relationship is hostile. Jesse thinks Rachel is strange and ungrateful. Rachel thinks Jesse looks down on her. But it doesn't take long for the hostility to change to a solid friendship. They both want something more, but each one thinks there is no way it can happen because of their past.

Angel is a sweet, smart dog who knows what needs to be done and does it. Once again, the dog is essential to the story. Without Angel, Jesse and Rachel might never have met.

My hope is this book has not only entertained you, but encouraged you as well. Remember, God can forgive you – no matter what you have done.

I love to hear from my readers. You can contact me at tina@tinamiddleton.net.

Turn the page for a sneak peek at the first chapter of *Unintended Target.*

May God bless you richly!
Tina Ann Middleton

The Forrestville Series
Book Three

Tina Ann Middleton

Publishing

Chapter One

"Surprise! Congratulations, Maggie!"

It seemed half of Forrestville had crammed into the party room at MaryAnn's Diner. Maggie looked around at the sea of faces with a big grin on her face and tears in her eyes. These people were her friends. More than that, many of them were like family to her.

"Cut the cake, Mom."

Robert vibrated with excitement as he stood next to his mother. Maggie couldn't believe how much he'd grown in the past month. At twelve, his head came to just above her shoulder. Now he stood beside her, eager to dig into the luscious cake MaryAnn had baked for the occasion.

Maggie handed him the knife.

"You cut the cake, son."

"Really?"

Robert gave her a surprised look.

"Sure, I think you'll do a great job."

The boy's chest puffed out just a bit. He bit his lip as he slowly and carefully slid the knife through the cake. After cutting several pieces, he carefully put them on plates and handed them to his mother, who handed them to the eager townspeople gathered around.

Esther and Stephen Abrams came to stand beside their police chief and friend.

"Maggie, we should be serving you. You're the guest of honor."

Maggie grinned and shook her head.

"Don't you remember? My duty is to 'serve and protect.'"

Stephen shot her a look.

"Cute. Come on. You're going to sit down while we bring you a piece of your cake and some punch. Or would you prefer coffee?"

Maggie conceded and stepped away from the table, watching with pride as Robert played the gracious host. He seemed to soak up the attention from the group around him while he cut and served the cake.

"Hey?"

She looked away from her son.

"Yes?"

Esther followed Maggie's gaze.

"Robert sure is growing up."

Maggie nodded.

"Yeah, he is. It's hard to believe he's already twelve."

Stephen laid his hand on Maggie's shoulder.

"You've done a great job raising him. He's a good kid. I know you're really proud of him."

Maggie watched Robert as he laughed and joked with those around him. She smiled at the sight of him whispering in a friend's ear and the two boys cracking up.

"I am very proud of him."

The party wound down about two hours later. Most of the townspeople had only come to shake hands with Maggie and congratulate her for capturing another dangerous criminal. They had already left. The group remaining in the party room were her closest friends.

Maggie felt a tug of regret as she looked around the room. It seemed everyone there was in a pair. Stephen and Esther sat hand-in-hand, her other hand cradling her baby bump. Jesse and Rachel sat nearby; his arm slung around her shoulders as they told about their honeymoon in the Ozarks. David and Christy stood at the refreshment table, helping to box up the remainder of the cake for Maggie to take home.

They were all couples. Maggie sighed. She couldn't help remembering a time when she was part of a couple. That was before everything fell apart. Now she was a single mom, trying her best to raise her son to be a godly and caring man. Their relationship was great. Both of them tried to be truthful and open with each other.

Maggie felt a twinge of guilt. She had been *mostly* truthful with her son. But there were some things he didn't know; and she would do her best to make sure he never found out.

"Maggie Jones, Police Chief in Forrestville, Louisiana Breaks Up Drug Ring."

Micky threw the newspaper onto the dirty floor and snatched up another one from a pile on the cluttered table.

"Forrestville Police Chief, Maggie Jones, Captures Industrial Spy."

He tossed that one on top of the first and picked up a yellowed piece of newsprint with a photograph of a female police officer, her face serious under her police cap. Walking to a dartboard hanging on the back of a closet door, Micky stuck the picture onto the board with a pin. Hatred smoldered in his dark eyes as he gathered three darts in his hand, then stood back to gaze at the picture.

A younger man sat on the tattered couch, listening as his companion ranted about the cop who had ruined his life. Although he kept a nonchalant appearance, Zach was quaking. This guy was nuts! Why was he still hanging around him?

"Maggie Jones, you ruined my life!"

Thwack! One of the darts stuck just to the left of the pictured face.

Zach could not answer the question of why he stayed, yet he felt reluctant to leave.

"Maggie Jones, I hate you."

Thwack! Another dart found its mark just below the picture.

Zach guessed he hung around because Micky was the only friend he had. Still, the ranting and talking about killing a cop were giving him the creeps. Maybe he'd just strike out on his own.

Before he could get up and slide out of the apartment, the older man turned and pinned him with a cold gaze. Zach couldn't seem to make his body work to get up off the couch and leave the apartment. After a long look at the younger man, Micky turned toward the picture, malice etched in his craggy features.

He stalked forward with the last dart held like a spear and stuck it directly into the heart of the young officer in the newspaper picture.

"Maggie Jones, I'm going to kill you."

Micky stared at the picture with the dart dug deep into it. Suddenly, he turned and snatched up a battered duffel bag. He began stuffing dirty clothes into it.

Zach watched him with a bewildered look on his face. He couldn't figure out what Mickey was up to and he wasn't sure he wanted to know. He slowly rose from the couch and began to sidle toward the door. Before he made it half-way his friend interrupted him.

"Where you goin'?"

Zach started. How did his friend know what he was thinking?"

"I, uh, I thought I'd step outside for some air."

The older man snorted and shook his head.

"We ain't got time for you to get no air."

Zach watched him roll another dirty shirt and cram it into the bag.

"H…how come?"

His friend gave him a leering grin.

"We're goin' on a little vacation."

Somehow, Zach knew they weren't going for rest and recreation.

"Yeah? Where we goin?"

The older man shot a dirty look at the newspaper picture fluttering on the dartboard.

"Forrestville, Louisiana. I want to pay a visit to an acquaintance of mine."

The Forrestville Series

Mistaken Target

Hidden Target

Unintended Target
(Anticipated release May 2021)

Remembered Target
(Anticipated release November 2021)

Made in the USA
Coppell, TX
27 May 2021